DYEING FOR CHANGE

AN ADDIE FOSTER MYSTERY

Kimberley O'Malley

Published by Carolina Blue Publishing, LLC

ISBN: 978-1-946682-13-0

To female friends, without whom I would have run screaming into the woods years ago. For understanding. For helping me to make sense of this crazy world. For having chocolate when I needed it most. For providing alcohol to go with the chocolate. But above all else, for providing a sympathetic ear, a shoulder to lean upon, a shared laugh or cry. I couldn't do this without you. I wouldn't want to. You know who you are.

Praise for
Kimberley O'Malley

Death Comes in Threes

"This was my first cozy mystery and I have to say I absolutely loved it. Kimberley did an amazing job at keeping me guessing what was coming next. I can't wait to see what happens between Addy and Detective Wolfe cause something has to happen between them! I also want to know who the man in Addy's dream is. And why those men were after her. Can't wait for the next book!"

-Under Cover Book Blog

"This was the first Cozy Mystery and Kimberley knocked it out of the park. I loved Addie and Grey and the two aunties. The detective puts out the vibe he is serious and hard core. But I am sure he has a soft spot for Addie. Hopefully in the next book we will see where the sparks fly for Addy and why these guys were after her. KUDOS to Kimberley for such a great read."

-Wanda Bridget Hickey, Verified Kindle customer

"This was my first Cozy Mystery and I loved it. I was drawn in by Addie and adored Grey. He was such a charming, funny and protective character. I can't wait to find out more in book two. This book is great for rainy days or a light read while you're on holiday."

-Author T. S. Petersen

Chapter One

Her breath lodged in her throat. She edged through the doorway into a darkened room, not knowing what she'd find there. Everything in her, from her shaky legs to her pounding heartbeat, screamed 'go back'! But she couldn't. Something compelled her forward. She slid her hand along the wall, searching for a light switch. Finding none, she inched ahead on leaden feet. A coppery scent reached her nostrils. Its unpleasant odor sent icy sweat trickling down her spine. Evil lurked within the darkness. Her foot caught something on the floor. She threw out her arms, wind milling them frantically to keep from falling.

Addie Foster pushed away the memory of last night's dream and played with the straw in her extra grand, super sweet, over the top iced coffee. She took a sip, cursing her BFF for introducing her to these drinks. They were dangerous to her waistline and her wallet. She fanned herself, thankful for the table's umbrella. The sweltering late summer sun would be brutal otherwise. Even first thing in the morning. Yet last night's dream left her chilled.

"Sorry I'm late," Grey said, joining her at the table. "Some mornings, I just can't pry myself out of that bed."

She didn't bring up the dream. Her first since three men came to town to kill her in July. She smiled instead. "What you really mean is that Jamie wouldn't let you go." She winked at him. "I can see where the turkey baster may never come into play." She and Greyson Waverly had been friends since single digits. They joked about having a child together if neither married by a certain age.

He took a sip of the drink she'd bought for him. "Can you blame him? I'm fabulous."

She laughed at his outrageous claim. "Yes, you are, my friend."

"Jamieson and I are having fun. I wouldn't say he's threatening the turkey baster. At least not this early into it."

She covered his hand with hers, giving it a squeeze. "Well, I like him. And I think you're good together. He puts up with your crap. And besides, I still have several years left of viable eggs."

"Yes, you do. And after that, there's technology."

She made a face. "Funny."

"You know I say that with love." He pulled his chair in closer to the table and lowered his voice. "Made any progress?"

"No," she replied in a flat tone. "Six weeks have passed, and I'm no closer to figuring out why those men wanted me dead. Or who fought so hard to keep me alive." She drummed her fingers on the table, her nails making a short tapping sound. Three dangerous criminals from halfway across the world descended upon sleepy little Ocean Grove, North Carolina, turning her life upside down. They intended to kill her. And almost did. Twice. All three died, two taken out by a mysterious stranger who stepped in to save her.

"Not for a lack of trying on your part."

She shook her head, tossing her ebony curls in the process. "I don't know what else to do, Grey. I've looked at it from all angles. It just doesn't make any sense."

"I don't suppose you asked a certain hunky detective for assistance." He wiggled his eyebrows at her.

"Just because you and Jamie are all happy together, doesn't mean the rest of the world has to be."

"I take it that's a no, then," he asked, tongue firmly implanted in cheek.

She played with her straw, not sure how to answer. "I haven't seen him since the day they found the last body." She received a note from her anonymous benefactor, assuring her safety. "Detective Wolfe wasn't pleased with how things played out."

"He just has his panties in a twist because someone else saved the day. He didn't get to be the hero."

She laughed. "I'm sure that's it." There had been a few odd moments, when he forgot to hide his emotions, that she thought he might be interested. But then the professional façade dropped back into place.

"Just because Detective Hottie hasn't said anything, doesn't mean he isn't thinking it. Go for it. What's the worst that could happen?"

She tapped a finger against her chin. "He could say no. He could laugh at me. He could run screaming from the room."

"Or he could say yes. Which might be the scariest possibility of all. Then, you'd have to risk your heart."

"You forget that I'm seeing someone. Not sure Noah would appreciate me asking out another man."

"Honey, y'all haven't had sex yet. And you've gone on five dates. That should tell you something."

"Grey! That's a terrible thing to say. Unlike you, I don't have sex on the first date." She grinned at him. "I'm a lady."

"And I'm easy. Not exactly news. Dr. Barrett isn't the guy for you. He's way too nice. And by nice, I mean boring."

"Noah is not boring. He's enthusiastic about his work." She slapped a hand over her mouth but couldn't stop the laughter from bubbling out. "Okay, he likes to talk about his work a lot. I can't be the only one not wanting to hear about boil lancing while I'm eating."

"That's just wrong."

"But he's passionate about it. I admire that." She held up a finger when Grey would have interrupted. "My life has been crazy this summer. They almost killed me. Twice. Some mystery man killed people to protect me. And I have no idea why. So, if Noah is a little less than thrilling, I'm okay with that."

"Adelaide Foster, you better not be crossing your fingers under the table."

She held up both hands. "Noah and I are hanging out, having a little fun. No one said anything about marriage."

"Does he know that? Because I've seen the way he looks at you. You can tell he has images of a white picket fence and two perfect children running through his head."

"Stop. He and I have been on exactly four official dates, five if you count the time I ran into him in the coffee shop."

"And now for the most important question. Is there a zing? And don't try to tell me you don't know what I'm talking about." He smirked before taking another sip.

She let out a breath, ruffling the curls over her forehead. "There isn't any zing. The last time I felt that was with, well, you know who."

"Detective Hottie, that's who."

"And that should tell you something. First, he thought I murdered someone. Then he can't let go of my being at the center of such a mystery. No, thanks. There may not be any zings, but Noah is a nice man who cares about me. I owe it to myself to see where this goes. And before you say another word about it,

I have to go." She pushed more curls out of her eyes. "This hair isn't going to cut itself.

She gathered her purse, slipping her phone into it. "I have an appointment at Dyeing for Change. And you have to open the store." She stood up and walked around the table. "I'll see you later," she said before kissing his cheek.

"You be careful," he advised.

"What's the worst that could happen? I've worn the same cut for years."

He pursed his lips. "You know better than to put that out into the universe. Especially the way your life is going."

She patted him on the head. "Good thing I'm not superstitious. See you later."

She headed for her appointment. Gwen Tucker, owner of Dyeing for Change, agreed to come in early to cut her hair before Addie went to work. Gwen was great that way, always willing to fit her in when she needed a cut. She tended to wait until she wanted to take a pair of scissors to her own hair to make an appointment. She loved her naturally curly hair but freely admitted it had a mind of its own. And right now, she needed Gwen to tame it.

Dyeing for Change sat right in town, only two blocks from the book store. One of the many things she loved about Ocean Grove. Everything she needed was right here. Her store, the fabulous coffee place, great little restaurants, and her hairdresser.

Gwen's thick New York accent never failed to crack her up. She'd shown up in town maybe five years ago, tired of snow and 'months of grey', rented a vacant storefront on Oak Street, and the rest was history. She catered to mostly an older clientele, Addie's aunties included. Both Clementine and Beatrice held standing Friday morning appointments for a wash and blow out.

Her great aunts loved the gossip as much as the personalized treatment they received.

She turned onto Oak Street, smiling at people she passed. Even though she may melt, Addie loved summer. And besides, Gwen always kept it nice and cool in the shop. Reaching the front door of Dyeing for Change, she grabbed the handle to open it. But it didn't budge. The sign on the door still read closed. Hmmm…

Cupping her hands to see better, Addie peeked inside. She caught a glimpse of Gwen ducking into the back room, so she knocked. And waited. Gwen often wore earbuds and rocked along to eighties hits. She knocked again, harder and longer this time. After a moment, the owner appeared in the door, shaking her head.

"I'm not open yet."

"I know. You were going to cut this mess before I go to work. Remember?"

Gwen's eyebrows pulled together. "Today?" She opened the door, but before Addie could say anything, Gwen pulled her inside. She then poked her head out and looked up and down the street. She relocked the door.

"Everything alright?"

"What? Yes, of course. Why wouldn't it be? Sorry I forgot. Luckily, I came in early to do inventory." She laughed, but it sounded high-pitched and forced.

"Ugh. That's the least favorite part of having my own business."

"Agreed. But it has to be done." She jumped when someone slammed a car door out in the street, dropping her keys. "Oh, I'm so clumsy some days." She bent to pick them up. "Why don't you take a seat at one of the sinks. I'll be right there." She scurried into the back room.

She watched her go, wondering about her mood. Gwen was usually the most laid-back woman she knew. She shrugged. Gwen would tell her if she wanted. She set her purse on a counter and took the seat next to it. She reclined and thought about all she had to do today.

A few moments later, she heard Gwen talking on the phone. Although she couldn't make out the words, the tone of her voice sounded angry. Not that she was listening, but sound carried in the empty shop.

The call ended, and Gwen appeared at the sink, tight smile on her face. She gestured with her cell before sliding it in her back pocket. "Sorry about that."

"That's okay. I took the time to plan my day. I can't wait to have less hair."

"Let's get you washed, then." She tucked a towel around Addie's neck before lowering the back of the chair. Then she turned on the water. "Let me know if it's too hot."

"This is my favorite part. If I had the time, and the money, I'd come every day just to have you wash my hair."

"Hmmm," responded the normally chatty woman.

Probably having an off day. Everyone did from time to time. She closed her eyes and let her do her magic. She tried to relax, but Gwen's fingers stabbed her head.

A doorbell chimed from the back room. Gwen cut off the water. "The delivery guy must be early. I'm so sorry, I'll be right back."

"No worries."

She hurried off, drying her hands on a towel. Addie used the ends of the towel around her neck to dry water in her ears. As she pulled the towel from her ears, she heard voices but once again not the actual words. Then a muffled sound, sort of like a thump sounded from the back room. *Must be getting some boxes delivered.*

She lay back in the chair to wait. She slid earbuds in and hit shuffle on her playlist. "It's Raining Men" by the Weather Girls boomed in her ears. Grey loved to add random songs to her playlist. She had a dinner date with Noah tonight. Did that warrant buying something new? Not that she needed an excuse to shop. But all the stores had their new fall stuff in. Hard to think of wearing that when the temperature remained in the nineties.

She glanced at her phone to check the time and texted Grey. *"Running a bit late. Will be there as soon as I can."*

She checked her email, answering one from The Aunties about Sunday dinner. They wanted Noah to come. Of course, they did. They swooned over Noah when he treated Addie a few weeks ago. Even asked about his marital status, much to her chagrin. She wasn't sure where things were headed with Noah, but she knew one thing. Bringing him to Sunday dinner would be the equivalent of picking wedding invitations. She typed out a reply, informing them she would bring Grey instead.

She glanced at the time again. Gwen had been gone for more than a few minutes. She sat up and listened more closely. Nothing. She pulled the towel from around her neck and dabbed at the ends of her soaking wet hair.

"Gwen?" she called out. And waited. But the other woman didn't answer her.

She stood, unsure what to do next. She walked towards the back room. "Gwen, are you okay?" The door stood partially opened. She knocked once. "Gwen, you're starting to freak me out." Her heart raced. She pushed open the door a little more. "Gwen?"

Darkness and silence greeted her. She felt for a switch as she toed open the door. A chill raced down her spine, and she couldn't blame wet hair or air conditioning. *This was just like her dream.*

"Gwen?" She snapped on the light. And looked down at Gwen lying way too still on the floor. Her hand flew to her mouth. Red spread across the light blue of her shirt. She knelt beside her, grabbing her hand. "Gwen, hold on. I'm getting help." She pulled her phone from her pocket and dialed 911.

"What's your emergency?"

"My friend has been stabbed. There's blood everywhere. Too much blood." She gave her location to the operator. She just hoped that help would get here in time to save her.

She held on to Gwen's hand as though doing so might keep her alive. She grabbed some towels from a basket and tried to slow the bleeding. But nothing stopped the tide of red that flowed from her body. She knelt there, trying to save Gwen while she prayed for the ambulance to arrive.

After what felt like a lifetime but was only a few minutes, the wail of emergency vehicles sounded, matching the thundering of Addie's heart. "Please hold on, Gwen. They're coming. Do you hear the sirens? They'll be here any second." She looked at her friend's too pale face and hoped she had seconds left.

Pounding on the front door caught her attention. "I'll be right back," she murmured. She ran into the front of the shop. Her fingers, slick with Gwen's blood, fumbled with the lock for a second. With one last twist, she unlocked the door and pulled it open. "Hurry!" she cried to the two men wearing navy blue jumpsuits. "She's in the back."

"Ms. Foster!" came a familiar voice from behind her. She didn't have to turn to know to whom the voice belonged. Detective Wolfe had returned to her life.

Chapter Two

Addie turned towards him, holding out blood-soaked hands. "You have to help her."

He closed the distance between them. "I will. But right now, she needs them more than she needs me." He placed his hands at the small of her back, directing her to one of the swivel chairs and pressed her gently into it. "Stay here. Please." Then he approached the back room.

Several more police cars, plus the van she recognized as their crime scene unit, screeched to a halt in the street. A group of people in uniform entered the shop. The reality of the situation hit her. And her vision started to darken at the edges. She squeezed her eyes shut and leaned her elbows on her knees, lowering her head. *Wasn't that what you were supposed to do if you felt faint?* She felt herself falling.

A distant voice reached her. "I've got you." She felt arms go around her and under her legs, lifting her. "Just don't throw up on me again. I bought new shoes." That voice could only belong to one man.

"I'm not sure it's possible to embarrass one's self that much in only one lifetime," she mumbled. She opened her eyes and looked straight into his dark ones. *Damn! He still had that Heathcliff thing going on. And the zings are back.*

"You must be feeling better if you can joke." He carried her into the bathroom. A woman wearing one of the blue jumpsuits followed them into the small room. He set her down onto the closed toilet. "Mary is going to take a sample, then you can wash up."

The young woman stepped forward. "Hi. I'm Mary Rogers with the crime scene unit. I'm going to swab some of the blood from your hands." She did just that, taking a few samples, placing each in its own sealed bag. She nodded and left the room.

She looked down at her feet. "Poor Gwen." She wanted to add that this couldn't be happening to *her* again, but that seemed selfish. She looked up at him. "Is she going to live? There was so much blood. She was still breathing when I let them in, but it didn't sound like good breathing. I mean healthy breathing." She stopped talking and thought about her own breathing. In. Out. "I babble when I'm nervous."

"I remember."

"I guess it hasn't been that long."

"Forty-three days." His eyes never left hers.

She held his gaze, feeling a warmth spread throughout her chest. Something more dangerous than zings. "Can I clean up now?"

"Of course. I'll be outside when you're ready to answer some questions." He nodded before leaving the bathroom.

She stood on shaky legs and approached the sink. Gwen's blood covered her, from her fingertips to her neck. She'd ruined her shirt, so she pulled it off and tossed it in the garbage. Her bra would have to do for now. Turning on the water, she hit the liquid soap dispenser several times and lathered her hands and arms. The water ran red and then pink. She watched it swirl down the drain. She closed her eyes, but the image of Gwen lying in a pool of her own blood haunted her. Tears rolled down her face until her whole body wracked with sobs.

A soft knock sounded at the door. "Ms. Foster, are you okay?"

She shook her head, knowing he couldn't see that. But it was the best she could do. A moment passed. Then the door opened a crack.

"I'm coming in."

She lifted her head. Their eyes met in the mirror. He shrugged out of his suit jacket, draping it over her shoulders. "Let me help you." He unbuttoned his cuffs and rolled up his sleeves before cupping some running water and rinsing her forearms. More pink tinged water slid down the drain. He applied more soap, rubbed her hands and arms, and repeated the whole thing again until the water finally ran clear. "I'll be right back."

When he left the room, she remembered to breathe. And inhaled the scent of him, clean and male, mixing with the coppery odor of blood. She turned her face, burying her nose in his jacket so that she only smelled him. And sobbed some more.

He came back in, closing the door with his hip. He used the towel he carried to dry her hands and arms, first one and then the other. Gently, as though made of spun glass. "You look good in my jacket. It brings out your eyes."

A sound came from her throat, half-sob, half-laugh. She gave him a half-smile. "Soon, all the top models will be wearing them."

"That's better. You're getting some color back in your face. I worried."

She straightened away from the sink. "I promised to not throw up on you. Again."

"That's not what concerned me."

He reached out one finger, tucking a wet tendril of hair behind her ear. It was an odd yet gentle action. Heat pooled low in her belly at his touch. Then she remembered what had brought him back into her life. "You have questions for me."

He held her gaze another moment before answering. "Let's go outside." He opened the door and motioned for her to proceed him.

Addie walked to the waiting area before taking a seat. He chose the one diagonal from her, away from the door. He sat facing her and reached for his pocket before frowning. "Uh, you have my notebook and pen." He pointed to his jacket, wrapped around her.

"Oh." She slid her hand into the inside pocket, pulling out the requested items. "Here you go." She noticed he didn't touch her when he took them.

"Thank you. Now, why don't you start from the beginning."

"I can't believe we're doing this again." She took a deep breath before telling him what happened.

"Are you a regular customer here?"

"Yes. Well, not really. What I mean is I have been coming here since she opened. But I only get a haircut, nothing fancy."

"But you always come here?"

"Yes. When I remember to get my hair cut." She brushed some out of her eyes and sighed. "All I managed today was to get it wet."

"I noticed she doesn't usually open until ten. Yet you were already here."

"I'm hopeless about remembering to get my hair cut. Gwen always fits me in last minute. To avoid disaster. Sometimes she opened early for me."

"Disaster?" One dark eyebrow, dissected by a scar, rose.

"Uh, cutting my own hair. I tried that. Once. Don't ever do it."

A soft chuckle escaped him. "I didn't plan to. Sounds dangerous."

"It wasn't pretty."

He jotted a few things, never breaking eye contact. "How well do you know Gwen?"

"Oh, pretty well. She and I." She stopped for a moment. "Actually, not that well at all. She's a very private person, but kind of sneaky about it."

"Sneaky? What do you mean?"

"Not in a bad way. But Gwen always asks her customers about themselves, their lives, families. Now that I think about it, she never talks about herself at all. I tried to get her to come to a book club meeting. I hold them monthly at the store."

"No go?"

She shook her head. "I even asked her to go have a drink, but she always made excuses. I stopped asking."

"But you continued to have her cut your hair."

"Well, sure. I didn't take it personally. And besides, my aunts would not be happy." She sucked in a sharp breath. "Oh no. My aunts will be devastated. They come here every Friday morning at ten like clockwork."

"Any chance they knew her better?

"No. We've talked about it a few times. How Gwen is super friendly but never talks about herself."

They both looked up at loud voices just outside the front window. She winced when she recognized Grey's.

"My best friend is in there. You have to let me through. Addie!" He waved at her while glowering at the cop stopping him.

She stood slowly, not wanting to hit the floor. Her legs shook but held her. She slid her arms into his jacket, thankful for the warmth. She doubted she'd ever feel warm again. "Do you need anything else from me, Detective? I'd really like to go home and take a shower. Grey can drive me."

He stood as well. "That's all for now. If I think of anything, I'll be in touch. You do the same."

"I will."

She started to remove his jacket, but he stopped her. "Keep it. I'll get it back from you another time."

She glanced down at herself, remembering she only wore her bra underneath. She pulled the lapels closer together. "Thank you. Can't risk being arrested for indecent exposure."

"There wouldn't be anything indecent about it. But I'd rather it not be on a public street." He gestured with his hand towards the front door. "After you."

"Let me get my purse." She walked over to the sinks and grabbed her purse. The side zipper gaped open, something she didn't remember doing. But then, she had sort of witnessed a brutal crime.

He held the door for her. "Oh my God, Addie!" Grey pulled her into his arms. "Are you okay? What happened?"

She peeked around his arm at the people gathered on the street. She didn't want to be a show for them. "Can you take me home, please? Now?"

"Of course, honey. Whatever you need." He narrowed his eyes. "Detective."

"Mr. Waverly."

"Thank you for taking care of my BFF. I've got her now."

"See that she gets home. She's in shock."

"I'll do that." He placed an arm around her shoulders. "My car is over there beyond the police tape. Let's go."

She murmured her agreement, allowing him to lead her towards his car. She glanced back at Detective Wolfe. His face closed once again, remained unreadable. The tender look he had given her in the bathroom only a memory.

Chapter Three

Addie groaned at the sight of Betsy, The Aunties' 1967 Cadillac, in her driveway. She loved them but could do without the inquisition. She turned to Grey. "Did you tell them about what happened?"

He pulled his car next to theirs and turned off the engine. "No, but they know more about what's going on in Ocean Grove than the mayor does."

She sighed. "That's true." She looked down at the detective's suit jacket she wore. "Going to be hard to explain this."

"I'm still waiting to hear that one." He waggled his eyebrows.

"I'm not doing the walk of shame. He gave it to me to wear because Gwen's blood soaked my shirt."

The expression fell from his face. "Right. Sorry." He got out and came around to help her. "Maybe they won't notice."

"Nice try." She led the way up the driveway, feet dragging with each step. She loved her aunts, but they exhausted her. And this day had taken everything out of her. Not to mention she hadn't slept well last night after the dream. She'd have to tell Grey about that. And probably Detective Wolfe.

They barely made it through the door before the assault began.

"Oh, my goodness! Are you all right?" This from Aunt Beatrice.

"Does this mean you'll be seeing that lovely detective again?" This from Clementine.

Luckily, the girls, her Shelties Lily and Gracey, met her with yips and kisses. She dropped to her knees, gathering their wiggling bodies in her arms. "Oh, hello, girls. Mommy's back." She normally took them to work but left them at home today because of the hair appointment.

"Young lady, we have questions," intoned Aunt Clementine, the sterner of the two.

Addie got up and collapsed on the couch. The dogs pressed in against her legs. "I don't know how Gwen is. She lost a lot of blood. They took her to the hospital. Yes, I'm fine. Yes, I saw Detective Wolfe."

"Have you told Dr. Barrett about what happened?"

She bit her lip. In all the confusion, she'd forgotten to call Noah. *Didn't that mean something?* "I'll text him. Let him know I'm okay." She stood. "More than anything, I need a shower and then a nap." She rubbed at the base of her skull. "And maybe some ibuprofen." She widened her eyes at Grey, who took the signal.

"Ladies let's clear out and give her a chance to breathe. Who should I call at the church about starting a prayer chain?"

"Oh, sister and I can take care of that, young man. Can't we, Beatrice?"

"Well, of course we can. We'll go home and start on that, right away."

Their voices faded as he led them out to the driveway. Addie walked into the kitchen. "Here you go, my good girls." She threw each a treat before heading into her bedroom. She removed his jacket, resisting the urge to sniff it one last time, and folded it over a chair. She made a mental note to clean it before returning it. It now held blood and more than its share of dog hair.

She stripped off the rest of her clothes and headed into the bathroom. She wasn't kidding about the shower. She couldn't help feeling like Lady Macbeth. Despite having scrubbed her hands and arms, she could still feel Gwen's blood on her. She turned the shower to as hot as she could stand it before ducking under the spray.

Silent tears coursed down her face, mixing with the water from the shower. So much of Gwen's blood had poured onto the floor of the back room. All color had leached from her face, leaving her looking more dead than alive. She could only hope they got her help in time.

She shampooed her hair and then washed her body. She used her loofah to scrub her hands and arms until they were red. She'd never feel clean again. She stood under the spray, only turning it off when it grew chilly. She stepped out and wrapped herself in an oversized towel. Swiping at the fogged mirror, she took a good look at herself. Red, puffy eyes greeted her. No surprise there. She held a hand to her head. She should have started with the ibuprofen.

Despite the time of year and hot shower, she hugged the towel closer to her. A chill seeped through to her bones. She ran her fingers through her wet hair and hung up her towel. Stepping back into her bedroom, she pulled on underwear and sweats. Then she headed into the kitchen.

The girls had been lying near the couch but ran to greet her. Dancing around her feet, they followed her as she made herself a hot chocolate. She'd be adding The Aunties' secret ingredient; a shot of Kahlua. So, what if it wasn't even noon? Grey would be sad when he found out she's drinking without him.

After stirring her drink, she carried it into the living room and curled up on the couch. *What was happening to her life?* Things had been going along quite nicely until July. Then the bottom dropped out. She started having dreams; scary ones that became her new reality. Woke her up in a cold sweat. Sometimes on the floor. And then they turned prophetic.

She held the hot mug in her hands, gathering strength from its warmth. She would get through this. After all, no one had tried to kill *her*. This time. Last night's dream had been vague, as they always were. She walked into an unfamiliar room, holding her hands out in front of her. They were covered in blood. Gwen hadn't appeared in it.

She took a sip and then ground her molars. Why have these dreams if she couldn't help anyone? But what if she'd seen Gwen in it? Would she have told her? Would the hairdresser have thought her mad? She blew out a pent-up breath. The ring tone Grey had assigned to Noah, the instrumental theme song from *Grey's Anatomy*, sounded, pulling her from her thoughts. She hesitated, not really wanting to speak with him. But manners won, and she hit accept.

"Hey, Noah." Even to her own ears, it sounded luke-warm at best.

"Addie, are you okay? I just heard."

"Oh, I'm fine, thanks. Maybe a bit shaky. How's Gwen?" She shuddered remembering the scene in the back room.

"I, uh, can't answer that. Patient confidentiality and all that."

She frowned. "I understand." And she did understand, but she needed to know.

"Do you want me to come over? I have a little free time. I could bring something for lunch."

She looked at her mug sitting on the coffee table. *It would be a liquid lunch for her today.* "No, thanks. I know you're busy. I have stuff here to eat."

"Well, if you're sure." He dragged out the last word a bit, as if trying to convince her.

"I am. Thank you, Noah. That's sweet. I need a nap."

"Are we still on for dinner?"

She stifled a groan. She should want to have dinner with her boyfriend. Or whatever he was. Detective Wolfe's dark, enigmatic eyes flashed in her mind. She shook her head. He was the last person she should be thinking about.

"Can I get back to you? Or maybe get a raincheck?"

"Oh. Sure. Let me know."

She hated hearing the disappointment in his voice. It felt like kicking a puppy. "I'm going to take a nap. I'll see how I feel." She crossed her fingers at the white lie. She wasn't having dinner with him tonight. Maybe never. Damn. Grey was right. Again.

"Okay. I'm being paged to the ER. I'll talk to you later. Enjoy your nap."

"Go see your patient." She hung up before he could say anything else. Also, probably not a good sign. Placing the phone on the coffee table, she finished her hot chocolate. The Kalua created a pleasant warmth in her belly.

She stretched out on the couch, trailing the fingers of one hand over the side to pet the girls. "He may not be the one for me. At least I still have you guys." She received doggy kisses in return. She snuggled down further, drifting to sleep. *No nightmares, please.*

*****

The insistent chime of the doorbell pulled her from a peaceful, and dreamless, sleep. She didn't open her eyes. Maybe they'd go away. Give up on her. A firm knock sounded.

"Ms. Foster? Are you in there?"

She bolted from the couch. And almost face planted. Perhaps less Kahlua next time. Straightening her wrinkled clothes, Addie rushed to the door. She opened it and took an involuntary step back at the sight of him. *Why couldn't Noah make her feel even half of that?*

"Detective Foster."

He dipped his head in that way of his. "Ms. Foster. May I come in?" His gaze swept over her, no doubt taking in her ratty old sweats. *Great!*

She stepped back to give him room. "Of course." She hadn't stepped back far enough. He passed within inches of her, sending her pulse rocketing. She closed the door and followed him into the living room.

Gracey and Lily, delighted with company, rushed him as soon as he sat in an armchair. She watched them wiggle against his legs, begging for a pat on the head. She understood that feeling. And because she did, she sat on the couch, as far away from him as possible, with her hands clenched in her lap.

He pet both of her dogs, scratching behind Lily's ears and the base of Gracey's tail. *How did he know that?* "Did you need something?" She winced at her tone.

He gave them each a final pat on the head. The girls came back to her, lying at her feet. He sat forward in his chair. "There's no good way to say this."

"Gwen died."

He nodded. "She lost too much blood at the scene."

Her chest ached at his words. "I think I already knew," she whispered. Her eyes burned with unshed tears.

"Is there anything else you can think of? Anything at all? Maybe a sound you heard? Something you may have smelled?"

"It all happened so fast. One minute she was wetting my hair, and then she was gone. I never should have put in my earbuds. I might have been able to save her."

He stood, pacing the room. "Absolutely not."

Her eyes widened. She jumped off the couch. "You can't know that."

He stopped within feet. "Whoever did this to her nicked her carotid artery. You could not have saved her."

"Maybe if I had gone to check on her sooner." The tears that had burned her eyes now flowed down her face. "I shouldn't have waited."

He grabbed her by the shoulders, shook her. "And what then? What if you had gone back there when the perp was still there?" His eyes blackened. "Then I might have found you dead on the floor as well."

Her breath caught. "I didn't think of that," she whispered, her voice shaking.

"Of course, you didn't. You never think of those things." His voice grew louder, bordered on yelling. "But I do."

She took a step back, sliding out from under his hands. "Why are you angry with me?"

And just like that, the fight left him. His shoulders slumped. He ran a hand through his short, dark hair. "I'm not angry." He sank back into the chair. "That could have been you on the floor. In a pool of your own blood. Then what would I have done?" He held her gaze, his eyes brimming with something.

She took a step toward him to say, well, something, when the doorbell rang. The girls barked hysterically. She silenced them with a hand signal. "I have no idea who that could be." She turned towards the door, but his hand on her arm stopped her.

"I'll get it. You can't be too careful."

She watched him approach the door, one hand on the gun he wore at his waist. She sat on the edge of the couch, one hand on each of her dog's collars. "It's okay, girls." She wasn't sure whom she was trying to comfort.

She heard the door open, followed by his deep voice. "May I help you?" And then Noah's voice asking for her. She swallowed. Hard. *This should be interesting.*

The two men entered the room. "Ms. Foster, your boyfriend is here." His words were clipped. "I can see you're in good hands. I'll see myself out." He left before she could say anything.

She watched him leave, shaking her head. *What just happened?*

Noah rushed towards her, a large bouquet of roses extended towards her. "I couldn't stay away." He looked her up and down, like any good doctor would do. "I'm so glad you're safe," he breathed before throwing his arms around her.

She waited for, hoped for, a zing. But none came. Why not? Noah Barrett was a good man. He saved lives, for goodness sake. Why couldn't she fall for *him*? Why did she have to have feelings for the dark, brooding, complicated one?

"I'm fine. Or at least I would be if you weren't holding me quite so tight."

He took the hint and let her go. "I'm sorry." A smile lit his face. He held out the flowers to her. "These are for you." And then that smile disappeared. "I don't know what I would have done if anything happened to you."

She sighed and took a seat. He said all the right things. Did all the right things. But they still lacked zing. And she didn't care for roses. But he had no way of knowing. "Thank you, they're beautiful. You shouldn't have." *You really shouldn't have.*

"Of course, I should have. You're my girlfriend. And you could have died."

He sounded sincere and so sweet, she couldn't tell him the truth. Not right now anyway. So, she sat back and listened to him go on about how he'd worried about her. And thought of another man. An intense, brooding one. Yep, she was going to Hell.

Chapter Four

The next day, Addie walked through the center of town, trying to enjoy the bright summer sun. But she couldn't shake the sadness, and horror, of Gwen's death. All around her, children splashed in the fountain, friends sat on benches chatting about their day, lovers held hands while they strolled. She shook her head, envying them. She ducked into the diner down the street to pick up their lunch orders. And immediately recognized her mistake.

"Honey, are you okay? Tell us what happened."

Madge, who had waitressed here as long as Addie could remember, pounced on her the second she walked in the door. The older woman wore her red hair, not a color found in nature, piled impossibly high on her head. That engineering trick must have required at least half a can of hair spray. Another of Gwen's customers.

"I'm fine, Madge. Thank you for asking. Can I, uh, get our order, please?"

"Oh sure, honey," she replied in a voice that spoke of her two pack a day for forty years habit.

She sat at the counter near the register and waited for their meals. And tried to ignore the curious stares. She should have let Grey come pick up the food.

"Hear you were with Gwen when she died. Starting to become a habit for you, isn't it?"

She swiveled on her seat, biting her tongue. Old Mr. Mc Manus, also known as the meanest person in Ocean Grove. She turned away, deciding to not dignify that with an answer.

"No need to get uppity, missy."

She swiveled back around and gave him her biggest, fakest smile. "You'll know when I'm uppity."

"Here you go, love."

She turned back to find Madge standing there, takeout bag in hand.

"That'll be $13.99."

Addie handed over her credit card and waited. She tucked it back in her wallet after Madge ran it and signed the receipt.

The waitress leaned in close. "Gwen did my hair as long as she's been here. I'm going to miss her." She patted the atrocity on top of her head. "Anything you can tell me about what happened?"

Great. "I can't really say, Madge. You know, because of the investigation."

The other woman's sucked in breath told her she'd taken the right tack. She patted her hand. "Sure. Of course."

She picked up the bag. "Thanks. See you soon."

She left the diner, thinking about what happened. People were curious, like they were a few weeks ago. When her life imploded. Or nosy, as Grey preferred. Her BFF had zero patience for idle gossip. Especially when it targeted her.

She stopped at the corner, waiting for the light to change, and squinted in the bright midday sun. Reaching up, she pulled down the sunglasses perched on her head. The light changed. As she started to cross, the sound of a motorcycle caught her attention.

Out of the corner of her eye, she saw a flash of movement. And felt a tug on her arm.

The man standing next to her grabbed her purse, trying to pull it from her arm. She yanked her arm back and threw the bag containing their lunch in his face. And then she shoved him. Hard. Which worked until he shoved back.

Next thing she knew, she landed on the ground. On her butt. The guy took off. People crowded around. She heard snatches of excited conversation.

"Call 9-1-1."

"Ma'am, are you alright?"

"You're not safe anywhere these days."

A hand reached down to help her up. She took it. "Thank you," she said to the older man standing there.

"I saw the whole thing. I can tell the police."

"Uh, that would be great."

She dusted off the seat of her capris. Her hands shook a bit, but it could have been worse. She moved over to a bench in the shade of a tree and sat. She really had the worse luck. Bystanders murmured around her, offering her everything from water to a ride home. She thanked each one and declined. After a few minutes, the wail of an approaching police car grew louder. It drew to the curb, and an officer got out. She closed her eyes on the dread of answering questions.

"Hey, I know you."

Addie looked up at the voice. Officer Natalie Burke, whom she'd met earlier this summer, approached her.

"We really have to stop meeting like this," she joked in return.

"What happened?"

She told her about the attempted mugging. "There were several people who saw everything. They might be able to tell you more."

"I stood right there, a few feet behind her, waiting for the light to change." This from the man who had helped her up.

"Thank you, sir. If you wouldn't mind waiting a few minutes, I'll be happy to take your statement."

"Of course, Officer."

"Addie, excuse me for a minute."

She watched as Natalie walked off a few steps and pulled her cell from her pocket. The conversation was brief, and she returned to her side.

"Did you get a good look at him?"

She shook her head. "Not really. It all happened so fast. He wore dark glasses and a baseball cap pulled low over his eyes."

"He wore jeans and a blue and green striped shirt, Officer."

Natalie turned once again to the Good Samaritan. "Thank you, sir. I'll be right with you."

"Are you injured?"

"Just my pride." She pointed into the street. "And my lunch. I threw it in his face."

"Good thinking. At least you still have your purse."

"That I do. I shoved him. I don't know what came over me. He made me so mad. I work hard. I'm not giving my purse to some guy just because he thought I made an easy mark."

"You've been watching TV police shows again, haven't you?"

She shrugged. "Maybe a few. Grey makes me."

The officer laughed.

A dark sedan pulled into the curb right in front of her. Detective Wolfe got out of it, looking perfect as usual. *How did he manage that in this heat?*

"Thank you for the heads up, Officer Burke. I can take it from here."

"You got it. I have a few witnesses to interview." She turned to Addie. "You take care."

"I will. Thanks again." She took a deep breath to quiet the herd of butterflies taking flight in her stomach.

"Ms. Foster."

"Detective Wolfe." He stood beside her, staring through reflective lenses. She wondered what he thought.

He heaved a sigh. "Can I give you a ride home?"

She stood, purse still clutched to her side. And lifted her chin. "No, thank you. I'm heading back to the bookstore." She started to move away from him, but he stepped in front of her.

"Don't be stubborn. Let me give you a ride."

She tilted her head up to look at him. "It's only two blocks." She stepped around him.

"Then I'll walk you there." He fell into step with her.

"Suit yourself." She walked off, knowing she sounded like a six-year-old. She couldn't help it. He brought out the worst in her. Made her want things. Things she should want with Noah. "Great," she muttered aloud. Now she had to tell her 'boyfriend' that something else happened to her. He'd be camped on her doorstep.

"What's wrong?"

She glanced at him, but the shades concealed his expression. "I can't talk to you when you're hiding."

He took off the sunglasses. "What's wrong?"

She faltered, almost stumbling. "Now I have to tell Noah that something else has happened to me. He already wants to wrap me in cotton." She glanced up at him in time to see his mouth tighten. And tried to not smile.

"I take it that's your boyfriend? Noah?"

She couldn't help it. Annoying him amused her. "Noah Barrett."

"The same Dr. Barret who treated you in the hospital? Isn't that against the rules?"

"He's not my doctor anymore. So, no."

"Well, it should be."

"I have bigger things to worry about. Don't you think?"

He turned his head to stare at her. For the length of several heartbeats. "Of course," he muttered and continued walking.

The journey to Smiling Dog Books consisted of less than two blocks. They finished it in silence. But not a comfortable one. At least not for her. His body, large and warm and smelling way better than she wished, stayed right next to hers. In step with hers. Their arms hung at their sides, hands almost, but not quite touching. Yet she could feel him as if wrapped in his embrace. The heat coming off him burned her. In the best way possible.

They stopped at the light across the street from her store. She stared at it, seeking comfort in the familiar. But the robin's egg blue exterior, with its bright window boxes of flowers in riotous colors, mocked her as her mind whirled in a thousand directions. *Why would someone kill Gwen? Had this been a random mugging or something more sinister? When would he ever kiss her?*

"No," she cried, shaking her head. She started across the street, but a firm hand on her arm stopped her. And a car whizzed by, blaring its horn.

"Where were you?" he muttered. Anger, or maybe concern, darkened his face.

"You don't want to know," she returned. She ducked her head, feeling the warmth spread across her face. Not a great time to think about kissing him.

He placed a hand under her chin, raising it until she looked him in the eye. That damn dimple appeared in one corner of his mouth, making him even more irresistible. "You might be surprised."

She continued to stare at him, lost in the depth of his dark eyes. They were warmer now, more like the color of dark chocolate. She felt the heat in them down to her toes, curling within her flats.

"Addie, were you planning to ever cross the street?"

Grey's amused voice equaled a bucket of ice-cold water. She turned to face the store. Her BFF stood there, hands on hips with a goofy smile on his face. She looked up and down the street before crossing, Detective Wolfe still at her side. But the moment vanished.

She sailed by Grey, glaring at him as she did. His smile remained in place. A blast of frigid air greeting her. She pulled her shirt from her sticky back, fanning herself.

A chorus of joyful yips and barks greeted her return. No matter what else happened, the girls were always glad to see her. She rounded the corner of the counter, bending down to hug Gracey and Lily. "Hello, girls. I'm back. Did you miss me?" They kissed her face and leaned into her body as if she just returned from war, not picking up lunch. Just another reason to love dogs.

She straightened up to find Grey and Detective Wolfe eyeing each other. *What was it with men?*

"Uh, did you forget something?" inquired Grey.

She stared at him. "Did I?"

He grinned at her. "You left to pick up our lunches."

"Oh, about that."

"What she's trying to not tell you is that Ms. Foster had another near miss." He turned to her.

"Maybe now isn't the best time, Detective Wolfe." She smiled, baring more teeth than necessary.

"What?" Grey looked back and forth between them, as though watching a tennis match. It might have been humorous if the situation differed.

"It was nothing."

"Someone tried to attack her."

They both replied at the same time, glaring at one another.

She sat down on the stool, leaning both elbows on the counter. "No big deal." Her quivering insides said otherwise.

Detective Wolfe let out a breath he seemed to be holding. "At the very least, someone attempted to mug you. But I'm afraid it was more than that."

Chapter Five

"What does that mean?" Grey stood, hands on hips, waiting for an answer.

She cringed as several customers turned curious glances their way. These two were worse than the toddlers who came to story time. She smiled at the customers. Then motioned for both men to approach the counter. "What is wrong with you guys?" she hissed at both.

"You need to take this seriously."

"When were you going to tell me?"

She rubbed her temples. She turned to Detective Wolfe first. "I do take it seriously. But that's my favorite purse. And I work hard for everything I have. I refused to let some random punk take it from me."

"But that's my point…"

She stopped him with a raised hand and turned to face Grey. "And as for you. I just walked in the door. The attempted mugging happened maybe thirty minutes ago."

"You could have called me. I would have come." He narrowed his eyes. "Did you call Noah?"

She laughed. She couldn't help it. "Of course not. He already wants to wrap me in bubble wrap."

As if this couldn't get any worse, the detective turned to her BFF. "Don't you think there's something wrong with a doctor dating one of his patients?"

"Former patient," she added through clenched teeth.

Grey shook his head. "Not really. The issue is that there isn't any zing. Noah doesn't stand a chance."

"Are you kidding me? I'm. Right. Here."

"You know it's the truth. What's the fun if there isn't a ny zing?"

"I'm never talking to you about that again."

"Interesting," Detective Wolfe added with a hint of a grin.

"Could we please get back to the subject at hand?"

Both men turned to face her.

"To be clear, someone tried to snatch my purse while I stood at the light. It wasn't a terrorist or international arms dealer. Just a guy trying to make a quick buck. I'm not in any danger."

Two brows raised, one blonde, the other dark and dissected by scar. *She really needed to ask him about that. Focus!*

The man in question leaned forward. "How do you know that for sure?"

"Why would you think I am?"

"Oh, I don't know. Maybe because you witnessed a brutal murder twenty-four hours ago?"

"He has a point."

"Whose side are you on?"

"Yours, always, as you know. But maybe we should listen to the man."

"Since when? You don't even like him."

"What did I ever do?"

"I never said that."

She held up both hands, wanting to bury her head in them. "Boys, we're off track again. A guy tried to mug me. He failed. I doubt he's going to come after me again. He'll find some little old lady who won't fight back. Which is terrible, so maybe go do your job and catch him."

"We don't know who killed Gwen or why. And you're the only witness. That alone puts you in danger."

"Now you tell me?"

"You were safe last night. I made sure of it."

She ignored the grin on Grey's face. And the warmth spreading in her belly. "What does that even mean?"

The slightest bit of red lit his cheekbones. "I, uh, may have been watching. The house."

"Oh." She didn't know what else to say to that but pressed a hand against her belly.

He cleared his throat. "Anyway, you're safe. For now. But I'd feel better if we knew why someone murdered Gwen."

"Do you have any leads?"

He shifted his weight. "I can't discuss that with you."

Grey laughed. "You obviously don't know her that well. Saying that will only set her off."

She sent him a look meant to squelch him, but he laughed again instead. "Ignore him."

"What does that mean? 'Set her off'?"

"Nothing."

"She has a curious mind. And the determination of a pit bull. She won't let this go. You may as well tell her what she wants to hear."

He turned back to her, pinning her with his dark gaze. "Listen closely. Do not poke your nose into this. Do not take chances. Do not get hurt. Again." His voice softened at the end.

Grey, for once, said nothing.

She toyed with an errant curl. "I don't go looking for trouble, by the way. It just sort of finds me."

He took a step closer to her until only the counter separated them. "Not this time. I can't worry about you like that again." He reached across the space between them, tucking that curl behind her ear. "Not this time." He never broke eye contact.

Neither did she. "You have ridiculously long lashes for a man. What a waste."

One side of his mouth raised. That dimple she longed to kiss. He turned on his heel and left.

She watched him leave without saying a single thing. And fanned herself instead. Then looked at Grey. "Not a word out of you."

He lasted all of three seconds. "Oh. My. God. I need Jamie to look at me that way. Well, okay, he does, but seriously. That man is hot. For you."

"I have to break up with Noah."

"Yeah, you do."

"There aren't any zings with Noah."

"Nope."

"And even though he's a nice guy -" She broke off when Grey raised a hand.

"Gonna stop you right there. Yes, Noah is a nice guy. But if that's the first thing you say about him, you have your answer."

She sighed. "I know. But the Aunties will be so disappointed."

"Also, not a good reason to stay with him."

"Agreed. But to be clear, I am breaking up with Noah because he's not right for me. Not because of Detective Wolfe."

He smirked. "If you say so."

"I do," she whispered in response. Then straightened her spine and resolve. "Now, go do something that qualifies as work."

He bowed deeply, tongue in cheek. "Yes, Master. And what will you be doing?" One brow arched above his bright blue eyes.

"Oh, nothing." She turned to her computer and pulled up her social media accounts.

"I don't even have to peek. You're researching Gwen, aren't you?"

She glanced over the laptop at him and smiled. "Are you still here?"

"Not anymore. One of us has to actually bring back lunch."

She waited until he left the shop before clicking onto the first of her apps. A few moments later, she'd not found anything about Gwen, just the shop. Gnawing on her lower lip, she pulled the stool over and sat, fingers flying over the keyboard.

When Grey reappeared more than thirty minutes later, she glanced up. "How is it possible that I can't find any trace of Gwen existing before she moved to Ocean Grove?"

"Maybe she was a ghost," offered a less than helpful Grey. He placed a shopping bag on the counter. "I got your favorite."

Her head popped up from the laptop. "You brought me mac and cheese? From Henri's?" She peeled off the lid and inhaled. "Oh, Grey, I take back every terrible thing I ever said about you."

"As if you would ever say anything less than stellar about me. And Henri insists you call it by its French name, macaroni au fromage. You know how he gets."

She nodded before scooping up a forkful and shoving it in her mouth. "Ummm," she murmured around the food.

"Good, I take it."

She swallowed before answering. "Winning the lottery is good. This is magnificent. Or magnifique, as Henri would insist.

How'd you get him to make it?" Henri, a true French chef, had trained in his native Paris. People came from miles away to eat at his bistro. But he wasn't exactly known for his personality.

He looked up from his salad. "I told him it was that time of the month and you needed comfort food."

She laughed, choking on a bite of her lunch. "I don't even care. Seeing yet another dead body is cause for comfort food." She coughed again. He handed her an unopened bottle of water.

"Tell me what you found out about Gwen. And don't bother telling me you didn't look." He waved his fork at her. "I know you way better than that."

"It's true." She took another bite, chewing and swallowing before she answered. "Gwen was probably in her forties, maybe even early fifties, yet I can't find one thing about her before she moved to Ocean Grove. That's only about five years ago."

"Well, we know she came from New York. As if being a rabid Yankees fan wasn't bad enough. She had that accent."

Addie tilted her head, remembering Gwen's accent. "That she did. But it was weird, don't you think?"

"What?"

"She never talked about anything that happened before moving here. Ever. No family photos in the shop."

"Well, you knew her better than I did."

She shook her head. "That's just it. I didn't know her beyond surface chat at the shop. I told the detective that she resisted any attempt I made at socializing. After a few times, I stopped trying."

"Maybe the Aunties know something. You know how they are."

She smiled. "You're right. Why didn't I think of that? If anyone could pry information out of someone, it would be Clem entine and Beatrice. I'll stop by there on my way home tonight. Maybe bring one of Gertie's pies."

"Ummm, pie. Now why did you have to mention that? A man has to watch his figure," he scolded.

"Very funny." She glanced at him. Not a spare ounce of fat on that one. She hated to think about his BMI. Certainly lower than hers.

"I'm not kidding. Jamie is younger than me."

They finished their lunches. Grey gathered their garbage and disposed of it.

The afternoon passed at a snail's pace. Addie put out new inventory and waited on the occasional customer. She itched to question her aunts about Gwen.

After she glanced at the clock for the hundredth time, he waved a hand in her direction. "Go ahead. I'll hold down the fort."

"Are you sure?"

"You're not going to be able to concentrate on anything here while you're wondering about Gwen."

She giggled. "You really do know me well."

"True. Too bad you're not famous. I could sell the details to the tabloids."

She screwed up her face. "Oh yeah. People would pay good money to know about Addie Foster, bookstore owner."

"I did say it was too bad you're not famous."

She whistled for the girls. Lily and Gracey raised their heads. "Who wants to go for a ride?" Any trace of sleepiness vanished at their favorite word. Both jumped up, crowding into her. She laughed at their enthusiasm. "Well, then, get your leashes." They each grabbed their own, blue for Lily and purple for Gracey. So much for being color blind.

"Thank you, Grey." She kissed his cheek before leaving.

She walked the length of the block, stopping before Any Way You Slice It. The bakery had been in the Sanders family for generations. The pink and purple striped awning always cheered her. As did Gertie Sanders, the current owner. She tied the girls to the metal ring in the wall placed for just that. She poured water in a travel bowl and set it down before patting both of their silky heads. "I'll be right back," she assured them.

The scent of cinnamon and other delicious ingredients teased her nose as soon as she pushed through the door. "Be right out," called her friend Gertie from the back.

"Take your time," she replied. "Sniffing the air doesn't add calories."

A laugh preceded her friend through the swinging doors. "Hey! If it isn't Ocean Grove's newest crime solver. How've you been?" Gertie came around the counter, hugging her. "But on a serious note, stop scaring me."

She hugged her back. Gertie was named for her Great Grandmother Gertrude, founder of the bakery. She laughed thinking about how people reacted when they met her. Gertie was in her late twenties and drop dead gorgeous. Her shining, blonde hair and clear blue eyes caught men's attention. Her petite, curvy figure kept it. Women wanted to hate her for these reasons. But they couldn't. Gertie possessed a sweet personality and would do anything for anyone. She drew people to her.

"Why does everyone think I go looking for trouble?"

"Well, you have seen more dead bodies in the past several weeks than most of us will in a lifetime." She crossed herself. "And I'm thankful for that."

"Trust me, it's nothing I asked for. But that's not why I'm here. I need something sweet for the Aunties."

Gertie laughed. "Ah, a bribe. Or repentance. What did you do this time?"

She crossed her fingers behind her back. The less people that knew, the better. "Nothing like that. I'm going for dinner and need something for dessert."

"Well, okay, then. One pie for the Aunties coming up. I know exactly what they need."

Addie watched as her friend pulled a pie from the display case and packaged it in their signature purple box, tying it with pink ribbon. She checked for drool, thinking about the pie contained within.

She handed over a twenty and took the box. "Are you at least going to tell me which one you picked?"

Gertie smirked and handed over her change. "Nope. Anticipation is half the fun."

"That's just mean."

"How are things going with the good doctor? You didn't think I'd let you go without details, did you?"

She placed the box on the counter to put away her change. And to give herself a moment to think of an answer. Always best to keep her hands busy.

"Nice stall tactic. You forget. I've known you my whole life. Out with it."

She laughed. "You're right, that's definitely my tell." She blew out a breath. "Not great. To be honest, I'm going to end it."

"What? Why? I've seen him. He's gorgeous. And a doctor."

"That sounded a bit dramatic on my part. We've only been on about five dates."

"Does that mean you've, uh, you know. Isn't three the magic number? It's been so long since my last date, I can't remember."

She made a face. "Why does everyone keep saying that? There isn't any zing. And he's too nice."

"Really? 'Too nice'? Although the lack of zing is a deal breaker."

"I know that sounds horrible. But he's so focused on me. Wants to only do the things I want to do. He never has an opinion of his own. And Grey says Noah is already picturing the white picket fence and children."

"Let me get my gun. He should be driven out of town."

"I know. I'm being ridiculous. But Grey isn't wrong. He does give off that vibe, already, like he's found his 'one'. And I'm not that person. And it's not fair to let him think that I am. So, I need to end it."

"You could always send him my way. I'm happy to comfort him," she quipped.

She picked up the box again and fished her keys from her pocket. "I'll keep that in mind. I have to get going."

Chapter Six

Gracey and Lily sat up in the back of the car as Addie pulled into the Aunties' driveway. She glanced in the rear-view mirror. Two tails wagged. Yips echoed throughout the car. "Who's a happy dog? You know the Aunties will rub your ears and fill your bellies with treats. Let's go." She grabbed her purse and the pie box from the floor on the passenger side. Because the driveway wrapped around the back of their old Victorian, she opened the hatch remotely, letting the girls jump out.

Clementine opened the back door. "Is that a box from Any Way You Slice It?"

She held the distinctive box aloft. "You know it is. However, that's all I know. Gertie wouldn't tell me what's in it. Said you'll love it though."

"Of course, we will." She patted her ample hips. "Does it look like I ever turn down one of Gertie's delicacies?"

The girls raced to the grass to do their thing, then dashed through the opened door. She could hear Beatrice opening their treat jar. "Sounds like Aunt Bea is about to spoil the girls again."

Her aunt shook her head. "Those dogs are so skinny, they'd blow away in a stiff wind."

Addie followed her into the house, not answering. The girls carried a healthy weight for their size. Only because she walked several miles a day with them. The Aunties were determined to feed them within an inch of their lives. Same for her.

"Hello, dear," called her Aunt Beatrice from the stove. "How was your day?"

She held in a laugh. Being here, in her childhood home, never failed to make her feel like one again. Especially when they pinched her cheeks. "Fine other than almost getting mugged." She wanted to clap a hand over her mouth.

But the expected clucking and worry never came.

"Oh, we know," answered Aunt Clementine as she set plates on the kitchen table. "Grey called us."

"Oh." *Grey called them? Why?*

"Yes, dear. He knew you wouldn't want to worry us. As if we don't already do that every day."

"It wasn't that big of a deal. I'm fine, and he didn't get my purse."

Clementine clucked her tongue. "What is this world coming to when a woman isn't safe in broad daylight?"

"Did they catch the scallywag?" asked Beatrice.

"No. At least not that I've heard."

Aunt Beatrice sighed, her ample bosom rising and falling with the effort. She placed a bowl of pasta on the table. "Is that yummy detective involved? He'll make it right."

She felt her cheeks warm at the mention of Jonah. That's how she thought of him, not Detective Wolfe. She turned away under the guise of getting silverware. The last thing she needed was the Aunties to see her blush at the mere mention of him. "I'm sure he will."

They sat down to eat, passing bowls of pasta and salad back and forth. Lily and Gracey lay on the floor on either side of Aunt Beatrice, probably hoping for some taste of dinner. "I'm sure they'll get him. It was a random thing."

She waited until after dinner to ask about Gwen. Aunt Clementine sliced the pie, apple berry as it turned out. She took a bite and smiled as the explosion of raspberry, blueberry, and apple, reached her taste buds. "Did Gwen ever talk to y'all about her life before she moved to Ocean Grove?"

Both Aunties shook their heads.

"And it's not like we didn't try to get it out of her," quipped Beatrice.

"Didn't you find that odd?"

"Everyone has secrets," added Clementine.

This wasn't going as she had hoped. "Did she ever mention any family? Or maybe where she lived up North?"

Aunt Clementine set down her fork. "You're trying to solve Gwen's murder." She rubbed her hands together. "How can we help?"

"Oh, yes. We'd love to help. Gwen was our friend." Beatrice patted her blue tinged hair helmet. "Where am I going to find someone else to do my hair just as I want it?"

And once again, she'd lost control of her aunts. "No, nothing like that." She crossed her fingers under the table. That's exactly what she wanted to do but wouldn't drag them into this with her. "Detective Wolfe asked me some questions, that's all."

"Oh."

"Too bad."

They answered too quickly for her comfort. "Don't get any ideas."

"Who, us?" they chorused, all wide-eyed.

She shook her head, fixing them with a stern look. "I'm serious, ladies."

"You're no fun," complained Clementine.

"Since you won't let us help with this, at least tell us about that yummy doctor you're seeing."

She took another bite of pie. "Noah is fine."

"He sure is," chortled Beatrice.

"Is he treating you well?" asked Clementine.

"Yes, of course." She finished swallowing the food in her mouth. "He's a perfect gentleman."

"That's disappointing."

"Aunt Beatrice!"

"What? I may be old, but I'm not dead. If he's a 'perfect gentleman', then you're not getting any."

"We've only been on five dates. Goodness."

"No sparks, huh? I had that happen once. Bummer," added Aunt Clementine.

"I thought three dates was the magic number," chimed in Aunt Beatrice.

She threw up her hands. "No, there isn't any zing."

"Dump him."

"There won't be any dumping, Aunt Clementine. I will let him know that we aren't compatible."

"Same as dumping."

She stood, taking her plate to the sink. "I'm done talking about this." She rinsed the dish before placing it in the dishwasher. Then she called the girls. "Thank you for dinner. We're going to go now."

"Don't get your knickers in a twist. We were trying to help."

A warmth spread in her chest. "I know you were. And I love both of you for it. Don't worry, I'll be fine."

"Of course, you will be, dear. But sister and I aren't getting any younger. We'd like some babies to spoil before we kick it."

"I'll keep that in mind." An image of a certain dark-eyed detective flashed before her. Better not to think about him right now. "Thank you for dinner." She kissed both of her great aunts before leaving.

She'd just put the girls in the back of the car and slid in behind the wheel when her phone rang. Grey's face flashed on the screen. She answered with a swipe of her finger. "Hey, great timing. I'm on my way home."

"What did you find out?"

"I'm fine, thanks. So are the Aunties."

"Sorry. I'm glad that's true. But I've been dying to hear what you discovered." He gave a short laugh. "Pardon the pun."

She groaned. Grey was famous, or infamous depending on your perspective, for bad puns. "Sorry to disappoint, but I came up empty."

"Nothing?"

"Nope. We all agreed that Gwen mastered at avoiding questions."

"Oh. What's plan B? You always have one."

"No idea. I thought for sure they'd have information. You know how they are." She heard a voice in the background. "Is that your other half calling you?"

"He is. See you tomorrow. Stay safe."

He disconnected before she could respond. "How about a walk?" she asked the girls. A chorus of excited yips answered her. "I'll take that as a yes."

She made the short drive home in under five minutes. After pulling in the driveway, she got out and let the girls out of the back. They raced to the door, chasing each other. She opened the door and turned off the alarm system. It had been her first purchase after a violent home invasion a few weeks prior.

"Okay, girls. Let me change, and then we'll go." She walked into her bedroom and changed out of her work clothes and into shorts and a T-shirt. She walked into the kitchen and grabbed her earbuds and a can of mace she kept in her junk drawer. Another thing she never would have bought before her life changed.

Lily and Gracey followed her to the door, circling around her as she sat to put on her sneakers. By the time she stood and grabbed their leashes, the girls had whipped themselves into a frenzy. Lily, always true to her herding instincts, grabbed at her laces.

She set the alarm, grabbed her keys and phone before setting out. After loading the girls into the car, she drove the few miles to Longwood Park. The girls stood, tails wagging as she turned off the car. "We're here, as you know." She got out and let them out of the back.

She plugged her earbuds into her phone and popped them in her ears. She tapped her 'exercise' playlist. Avicii's "Wake Me Up" started, and they set off at a brisk pace.

Within a few moments, sweat formed on her forehead and down the middle of her back. Welcome to summer in North Carolina. She felt better about the huge piece of pie she'd eaten. She started out at a brisk pace. The girls strained at their leashes as they passed the playground. A dozen children shrieked as they swung on swings or flew down slides. She grinned at the sight of them, trying to ignore the slight pang in her chest.

"Let's take the path, girls." The paved path wound in and out of trees. Depending on the route she chose, they could walk a mile or longer. She set out to the right, the longest way. She could use the one point five miles after that dinner. And the girls each had eaten more than their share of treats.

The setting sun filtered through the trees, leaving odd shadows here and there. She stopped to retie her sneaker. A loud crack sounded behind her, raising the hairs on the back of her neck. Both Shelties whined. She whirled around but didn't see anything. "Let's go, girls." She picked up her pace.

Rounding the next bend, they started into the thickest part of the woods. They hadn't passed another soul, odd for a summer evening. She pulled out her earbuds and tucked them into the neck of her shirt. Even the birds and woodland creatures seemed quieter than usual. Her heart slammed in her chest. She clutched the leashes tighter in her left hand. Reaching into the pocket of her shorts with her other hand, she clutched the canister of mace. She'd bought it hoping to never use it. An insurance policy of sorts.

Addie looked behind her. No one on the trail. She turned forward. No one there either. Yet she didn't feel any safer. Goose-bumps raised on her arms. *Someone's walking on your grave.* She could hear her mother's voice in her head.

Gracey flattened her ears against her head. Lily tucked her tail in-between her legs. She needed to stop this foolishness. The girls didn't need her sending her anxiety down the leash to them, making them skittish. "It's okay, girls. Mom's just being silly." She looked up and down the trail again. More bad luck. She'd reached the middle of it, so going back or forward meant the same distance.

But the tree cover grew thicker on this part of the trail. At this time of night, very little sunshine peeked through. Back the way they came, then. "Let's go, girls." She stepped up her pace until she jogged. The girls trotted beside her, heads turning this way and that, as though scoping out the landscape.

Her breath grew ragged, whether from exertion or fear she didn't know. A stitch developed in her side. But she pushed these thoughts aside. She'd deal with that when she made it back to her car. Safe with the doors locked.

They broke out of the heavily wooded section, now closer to the car. But her relief was short-lived. The sun had nearly set, and light faded by the moment. "Almost there," she told the girls, hoping to calm all three of them.

When every breath burned, she slowed her pace. They drew abreast of the now deserted playground. The wind picked up, sending the empty swings into motion. Without the sounds of small children laughing and playing, the scene held an ominous tone.

Almost there. Less than a quarter-mile to the safety of her car. She reached into her pocket for her keys, lacing them through her fingers. Gracey whined deep in her throat, the sound raising the hairs on the back of Addie's neck. She remembered the last time she'd heard her dog make that noise. A dead body had been involved.

She picked up her pace again, focused on reaching her car. Rounding the last corner, the sight of her car in the now empty parking lot flooded over her in a wave of relief. *They'd made it.*

The growl of a motorcycle, careening towards her across the lot, shattered that thought. She stood, frozen to the spot. Two men sat astride the machine. It screeched to a halt next to her, and the man on the back jumped off. He closed the distance between them. Without a helmet, she could see the same man who tried to grab her purse earlier today.

"Give it to me, and no one has to get hurt," he growled at her.

Chapter Seven

Her mouth dried. Lily barked at the man. Gracey growled. She clutched her keys until the metal bit into her hand. "Wh-wh-what are you talking about?" She stared at him, committing the details of his face to memory. In case she survived.

A cruel smile split his face. "Don't play stupid with me. I know Diana gave you something in the shop that morning. Hand it over." He took another step closer to her, his hot breath spilling across her face.

"Diana?"

"The hairdresser. The one who met a nasty end." His grin displayed perfect white teeth. Yet its sinister glint sent shivers down her spine. "I know you have something that belongs to us."

She took a step back while pulling on the leashes. She had to get the girls behind her. But Gracey had another idea. Lunging forward, she grabbed ahold of his leg, growling.

"Get that mutt off me." He swore under his breath, hopping on one foot. Before she could react, he reached down and grabbed Gracey. The dog released her grip. Addie watched in horror as he threw Gracey to the gravel. She let out one sharp yip, then lay still. Too still.

Ice settled in her chest at the sight. Then fear became anger. She dropped her keys, shoving her hand in her pocket. She grabbed the canister of mace and pulled it out. Aiming it at his face, she sprayed. "You monster! She's just a little dog."

His hands came up as he yelled garbled words. While he was blinded, she kicked out, striking him in the knee. He howled in pain.

The next few moments passed in a blur. The other guy jumped off the bike. He grabbed her assailant, helping him on to the motorcycle. The two roared off in a cloud of gravel and dust.

She dropped down next to Gracey. Lily already lay there, whimpering and licking the other dog's face. She stroked one hand over her head. "Hang on, sweetie. I'm going to get you help."

After unlocking her car, she lifted the small dog in her arms and placed her on the back seat. Lily jumped onto the floor below Gracey, continuing to whine. Her small pink tongue darted out, licking her sister. "You're a good girl, Lily. Don't worry. She'll be okay."

Darkness settled fully by the time she slid behind the wheel. She placed her phone in the holder and hit Grey's number. It rang several times. "Come on, Grey. Pick up. Pick up." It went to voicemail.

"Grey, I'm on my way to the emergency vet. There's been an accident. Gracey isn't waking up." She broke off, sobs filled the car. "I, uh, I don't know if she's alive or not. I have to go."

She raced out of the lot. On the street, she made a right and headed for the county vet. Although she didn't frequent this practice, they did have a vet on duty 24/7. At a red light, she glanced into the back seat. Her heart squeezed at the sight of Lily sitting on the floor with her face right alongside Gracey's on the seat. Gracey's side moved up and down, so she was at least breathing. "Hang in there, girl. We're almost there."

She hit another preset number as the light changed. "Detective Wolfe, this is Addie Foster. I, uh, have to talk to you. Something happened to me and Gracey. I have to take care of her first." Another sob broke free, and she grabbed a tissue. Not knowing what else to say, she disconnected.

The clinic appeared up ahead. She turned in, pulling into a parking spot. Jumping out of the car, she opened the back door. Lily lifted her head, seemingly pleading with her dark eyes for Addie to help her sister. "We're going to get her help. Don't worry, Lily."

She picked Gracey up in her arms. The dog groaned but didn't open her eyes. Whistling for Lily to follow, she kicked the door shut and bounded through the front door. "Help me," she cried. The young woman behind the desk picked up the phone and spoke a few words into it before coming around the corner of the desk.

"What happened?"

"A man hurt her." Tears ran down her face. "He p-p-picked her up and th-th-threw her to the ground. She won't open her eyes or respond to me."

Two others, dressed in scrubs, came through the swinging door to the back. They carried a small stretcher. She laid Gracey on it, and they disappeared into the back. Addie stared at the closed doors, letting the tears flow.

There was nothing left to do. Her legs shook, threatening to not hold her up anymore. She walked across the room and collapsed into a chair. Lily climbed up into her lap, placing kisses on her chin and hands. She wrapped her arms around the trembling dog, her tears soaking the soft fur of her back and neck.

She felt a presence next to her. The young woman from the desk smiled at her. "The doctors here are really good. Your dog is in good hands." She placed a clipboard on the chair next to her. "No hurry. Fill it out when you have a chance." She walked back to the desk to answer the ringing phone.

She buried her face back in Lily's fur, trying to pull herself together. Inhale. Exhale. Repeat. Time passed. She waited for someone to update her on Gracey's condition. She lost track of how long she'd been there when she felt someone take the seat next to her. Warmth flowed through her. Only one person caused that.

"Hello, Detective Wolfe," she whispered, not bothering to lift her head.

"I'm sorry about Gracey. Have you heard anything yet?"

"No," she sniffed.

"When you're ready, tell me what happened."

She felt him move closer to her so that his leg pressed against hers. Instead of the usual spark, she felt comfort. And peace. And safety. It broke the dam wide open. "We were walking in Longwood Park. The way the Aunties feed us, a daily walk keeps us healthy. I went down the path I always take. I thought the purse snatcher guy was a one-off. You know? A random thing."

"Wait. What?"

She lifted her head, turned and looked at him. His face loomed inches from hers. His brown eyes alert yet holding a touch of sympathy. "The same guy who tried to take my purse yesterday attacked us. And the guy on the motorcycle. I remember hearing it right before he grabbed for my purse. I just didn't put them together at that time."

"Stop. I need you to take it from the top. Tell me exactly what happened. Take your time."

She took a deep breath and told him everything. She halted when she got to their fight in the parking lot. "He didn't have to hurt her. She weighs all of seventeen pounds soaking wet. Although she did get a piece of him." She put her fist to her mouth, stifled a sob. "Then he grabbed her. And he thr-thr-threw her to the ground. She didn't move. She's never that still."

Lily pressed in even closer to her, lending support. "But I got him. Right in the face with my mace. Grey will be so proud. Oh, and I kicked him too."

He smothered a laugh. "Good for you. You did what you had to do to survive." He let out a shaky breath. "That was a little too close."

"You think?" She clasped her hands together. "I feel like crap."

"It's the adrenaline. Takes you up, then drops you like a rock." He placed one large hand over both of hers. "You should know that by now."

One corner of her mouth lifted. "True. The last few weeks have been, uh, interesting."

He barked out a short laugh. "That's one way of putting it."

A man in a white coat over dark blue scrubs came out through the swinging doors. "Ms. Foster?"

"Yes." She placed Lily on the floor, holding on to her leash. "How's Gracey? Is she..."

She swallowed hard, unable to even utter the word.

"I'm Dr. Vance. Gracey is resting. We can go back to see her, and I'll tell you about her injuries."

"Oh, thank goodness. I'd love to see her." She looked down at Lily. "Can I bring her? They're sisters."

"Maybe tomorrow. Gracey needs to rest tonight."

"Oh." She looked down at Lily, unsure what to do with her.

Detective Wolfe reached out and took the leash from her hand. "I'll stay with her. You go ahead." He sat on the bench, patting his leg. Lily went right to him, sitting and putting one paw on his knee. "Good girl." He reached down, rubbing her silky ears. "You've had a tough night, haven't you, little girl?"

She smiled at the big man talking to her little dog. Her heart did a funny tumble in her chest. "Thank you."

"No worries." He pulled out his phone from his suit pocket and gave some orders to someone named Dave.

"Okay, Dr. Vance. I'd love to see Gracey."

He led the way to the back. She gasped when she saw her poor little dog lying in a cage. A tube ran from a bag of fluids to her leg. She linked her fingers in the gate. "Hello, sweetie. Mommy's here." A brief wag of her tail rewarded her.

"She's groggy from the medicine we gave to sedate her. She has a bruised lung and a few cracked ribs. All in all, she got off lucky. It could have been much worse."

He opened the cage door. "You can pet her. Don't be afraid. Just don't rile her up too much."

She hugged him. "Thank you," she cried into his chest. Addie straightened up, wiping her eyes. "I'm so sorry. I don't usually hug total strangers."

"I'm not one to turn down a hug from a pretty woman." He smiled down at her. "Gracey can probably go home tomorrow or the next day. I'll be in my office if you have any questions."

She turned to face her dog. "Oh, Gracey. You were so brave. Mommy loves you so much." She stroked the white blaze that ran down the middle of her face. Her tail with the white tip brushed across the floor of the cage. Her eyes remained closed. She kissed her silky face before shutting the door. "You be a good girl. I'll be back tomorrow to see you. Sleep well, little one."

She walked to the swinging doors and stopped before them. And it all came crashing down. The fear. The guilt at Gracey getting hurt trying to protect her. Finding Gwen dying in the back room. She turned into the wall, leaning her head against it, and let the tears come. Sobs racked her body. She'd never been a pretty crier. She didn't care.

After a few moments, the door opened, and a wet nose pressed against her bare calf. Then strong arms turned her from the wall and into him. "It's okay. I've got you."

He'd taken off his suit coat and rolled up his sleeves. His warmth and spicy scent surrounded her, comforted her. "How could I not know anything about her? She was my friend. At least I thought so. Now she's gone. And I'll never know." The tears continued, burning her eyes. Her nose ran, and she sniffed. "I'm a mess," she muttered into his chest.

A handkerchief appeared in her line of vision. "Thanks." She blew her nose. Another thing she didn't do prettily. She'd be embarrassed later.

"Feeling up to a few more questions?"

She nodded and walked through the door he held open. She sat and whistled for Lily. The little dog jumped into her arms.

Detective Wolfe pulled up a chair facing her. His suit coat draped over the back of it. "I sent some officers and our crime scene techs out to the park. They didn't find anything. I'm disappointed but not surprised." He lifted one shoulder and let it fall. "Had to try."

"Of course."

"Do you remember what he looked like?"

"I'll never forget. He was taller than me but shorter than you. I didn't have to look as far up to see him. He had close cropped blond hair and hard blue eyes. And perfect teeth. He wore tan cargo pants, a long-sleeved green tee, and scuffed black leather boots." She held out both hands in front of her. "He had a tattoo on his left wrist. It looked like a lightning bolt, but it was mostly covered by his shirt, so I can't be sure. I didn't see any jewelry or scars." She sat back and took a blew out a breath.

"Eyewitness accounts are not usually that specific."

"He hurt Gracey. I'm not likely to forget. He's not getting away with this."

"Not to mention threatening you." His dark eyes warmed, setting loose the butterflies in her stomach. "Take me through the conversation again."

"He called her Diana, not Gwen, which didn't make any sense. And he kept insisting that she'd given me something." She closed her eyes for a moment, remembering the conversation. "First he said, 'Give it to me, and no one has to get hurt.' I didn't know what he meant. Then he said, 'I know you have something that belongs to us.' He insisted Diana had given me something. Gwen didn't give me anything." She closed her eyes. "He didn't have to hurt Gracey."

He squeezed one of her hands. "No, he didn't. We'll get him, Ms. Foster. But I need you to think about what he said. Is there a chance that she did give you something? Maybe a letter or piece of paper?"

She opened her eyes, looking into his. And shook her head. "We really weren't that close, now that I look back. We never grabbed dinner or saw a movie, despite my asking. She never came to my house, nor did I go to hers."

He ran a hand through his hair. "Think. How could she possibly have given you something? It must have been the morning she died."

She sat up straight. Lily jumped to the floor. "My purse!" she blurted. She stood, pacing the small waiting room. Lily shadowed her, tail up, ears forward. "We were at the sinks. My purse sat on the counter next to me. Maybe…"

"Maybe she slipped something into it. Is it the same purse he tried to snatch? You women tend to have more than one."

She laughed at that and sat back down on the bench in front of him. "And how do you know about women's purses?"

"I have sisters and a mother. I know things."

"Huh."

His eyes darkened. "What? Is it so strange that I have a family?"

No wife? She shook off that thought. None of her business. "You know everything about me. And all I know is your name and job title. And that dogs like you."

That made him smile. And out popped the dimple from her fantasies. "That's more than some people know about me."

She frowned at that. "And yet you know everything about me. Hardly seems fair."

He leaned in, crowding her a bit. "I only know the things about you I needed for my job. I don't know the important things."

Her heart became a humming bird, beating in her chest. "Ask me anything. I'm an open book."

He grabbed her wrist, one finger over her thrumming pulse. "Does Dr. Barrett make your heart race like this?"

Chapter Eight

Addie felt her cheeks warm. She pulled her hand from his but held his gaze even while she wanted to look anywhere else. "No," she whispered.

"Then why are you with him?"

"I'm not. I mean I am, but we've only been on a few dates." She dropped her gaze, focusing on the length of Lily's leash in her hands.

"Hmmm."

That brought her head up. Desire smoldered in his eyes. "Oh." If she could kick herself, she would have. *Oh? That's all she could come up with?*

One corner of his mouth lifted. "Is that a good oh or a bad oh?" He held up a hand. "Don't answer that. Not until you're no longer involved in one of my cases."

"Do you think that day will ever arrive?"

"I hope so." He cleared his throat. "We should check your purse." He stood, bending to brush some of Lily's hair off his pants.

She winced. "Sorry about that."

He shrugged one huge shoulder. "If it bothered me, I wouldn't pet her." He leaned down and stroked her head. "More than worth the price of dry cleaning. If you're ready to leave, I'll follow you home."

She tried to remember if she'd put away her laundry, then let it go. He didn't care about that. She stood, signaling Lily they were leaving. "I'm ready."

He held the door for her, winning more points he didn't need. His department-issued sedan sat next to her small SUV in the parking lot. He waited until she got Lily in the back and then herself before getting into his car.

On the short drive home, she glanced into the rear-view mirror more times than she could count. Knowing he tailed her made her feel safe. The thought of those men still lurking around kept her on edge. Detective Wolfe made her feel other things as well. But he made sense. Best to put that on the back burner for now. But knowing that didn't make it any easier.

Grey called as she pulled into her driveway. He'd never been known for his timing. She hit decline and texted him that she'd call when she could but that everything was okay. She jumped when knuckles rapped on her window. She grabbed her phone and keys before getting out.

"Sorry. Grey called me back. I sent him a text letting him know we're okay." She went to the back of the car and let Lily out. She ran right to the grass and squatted.

"She's well-trained," he observed.

As if knowing he mentioned her, Lily ran right up to him and sat, leaning against his leg.

"More dog hair." She walked to the front door and opened it, the other two following her inside.

"Don't mind the mess," she yelled over the sound of the alarm. She hurried to the key pad to turn it off.

"Good. You took my advice." He shut the door and leaned down to unclip Lily from her leash.

"I did. Right after the last incident." Funny word for almost dying. Twice. "I'll grab my purse." She dashed into her bedroom, returning a moment later with her purse. She held it out to him. "Here you go."

He shuffled his feet. "Uh, maybe you could look in it, see if there's anything that doesn't belong to you."

She giggled. "The big, bad Detective Wolfe is afraid to look in my purse? What do you think you're going to find?" Then she remembered the condoms Grey had given her. Just in case. And pulled it back towards her. "On the other hand, I'm happy to do it." She moved to the couch and placed it on her lap.

"Judging from your expression, I'm sorry I said no. And for the record, I wasn't afraid. It's about respect."

"Oh," she muttered. Would there ever be a time when she didn't put her foot in her mouth around him? She opened the main zipper and pulled out the bigger items to see better. Nothing she didn't expect to find.

"You say that a lot."

She raised her head. "You weren't supposed to notice." She unzipped an outer, rarely used compartment. It was tiny and didn't really fit anything, so she didn't expect to find something. And then she felt something hard. "Uh, there's something here." She slid two fingers down into the tight space and pulled up a flash drive.

"Not yours, I'm guessing."

"No. I never put anything in that pocket.' She held it out for him to take, but he held out a finger.

"I'll be right back." He dashed outside. She heard the beep of him unlocking his car. He came back in a flash, holding an evidence bag.

She dropped it in, frowning. "Sorry. I shouldn't have touched it."

"No worries. We have your prints on file from last time. Besides, it may only contain Gwen's. Or Diana's. Whatever her name really is." He sealed the bag and wrote on it while she watched.

"I hope that helps. I can't imagine that they killed Gwen for whatever is on it." She shuddered, remembering her friend lying in a pool of her own blood.

"You'd be surprised" He took a step closer. "I'll give it to our tech guy. He's amazing. If there's anything of interest on it, he'll find it." He pulled his keys from his pants pocket, jingling them in one hand. "I should get going." He glanced at the couch. "Will you be okay? Alone?"

"Oh, sure. I have the alarm system. And I won't be alone."

One dark eyebrow met his hairline. "Oh? I didn't realize."

She grinned. "Lily will be here. She may be small, but she's mighty. And she doesn't sound so small from outside."

Lily ran around the living room, barking, as if she knew they were discussing her bravery.

"Yes, I can see how someone with a gun might give it a second thought."

"Grey will come if I ask him. Or you could park a patrol car outside. That might deter someone."

"We don't really have the budget for that."

"Oh, sure. I'll be okay."

"I could come back. Uh, sleep on your couch."

Tempting. "I'll be okay."

"All right. But call Grey. I'd feel better knowing you're not alone." He started to leave, then turned back. "Just make sure it's not Noah staying with you." He left before she could respond.

She picked her jaw up from the ground. And called Grey. He answered on the first ring.

"It's about time. What in the blue blazes happened? And never, ever leave me a message like that again. Ten years, Addie, right off the top of my life."

She laughed, drawing strength from the normalcy of the conversation.

"I'm so sorry. It all happened so fast. I have a lot to tell you, but first I have a favor. Can you stay here tonight? Please?"

"On my way. Just let me call Jamie and tell him I won't be by. Give me thirty minutes."

"Thanks! And grab a pizza."

"One large with pineapple. Got it. See you soon."

She set her phone on the coffee table and walked to the door, locking it. She considered taking a shower but decided against it until Grey arrived. She remembered last time, when an arms dealer broke into her house while she showered. No need to repeat that.

"Who's hungry?"

Lily jumped to her feet and followed her into the kitchen, twirling in circles around her. She filled her bowl and set it on the place mat on the floor. Lily sniffed at it but backed away without eating.

She reached down and stroked her ears. "Poor girl. You miss your sister, don't you? She'll be home soon. Maybe some pizza crust will tempt your tummy."

She walked into her bedroom and pulled on a sweatshirt against the air conditioning. Or maybe the jitters from earlier. Her life had taken a weird turn. Again. A few short weeks ago, she'd been just another small town, small business owner. Her days screamed normal, boring even, to the outside observer. But she'd been targeted by international criminals who tried to kill her twice, witnessed a murder, and once again found herself in the thick of it. And still had no idea why.

This latest series of events seemed to have started with wrong place, wrong time. Not that it mattered. Danger still plagued her. But the real issue remained. What had happened in July and why? Even though all three had been killed, the doubts, in the form of an icy finger niggling at the base of her brain, remained.

She wandered back into the living room with Lily her faithful shadow. Curling up on the couch, she patted her leg. Lily jumped up, winding her small body against her mistress, resting her face on Addie's thigh. She stroked a silky ear and clicked on her Netflix app on her tablet. May as well watch that hunky Jensen Ackles solve an other worldly mystery while she waited for Grey.

But as gorgeous as she found her future husband, her mind whirled, making it impossible to concentrate on the story line. 'You're safe now' her mystery protector had told her via a note slipped in her mail. Mere minutes later, police discovered the third thug, shot to death in a car. His murder remained unsolved.

She wasn't any closer to figuring out the identity of this mystery person. Her what? Protector? Benefactor? No, that made her sound like an eighteenth-century orphan. Someone went through a lot of trouble to keep her safe. But also to keep his, or her, identity a secret. Why?

She turned her attention back to the screen. Even if she couldn't pay attention, a little eye candy never hurt. She played with the long, silky hairs around Lily's ears as she watched. Her dog made cute little noises in her throat, almost a humming. Canine for 'I'll let you do that for another hour.'

She made it almost the whole way through an episode when she heard a series of knocks on the front door. Two followed by a pause, and then another three. Grey developed this code after the first 'incident'. Lily stood on the couch, ears forward as if also listening. Quieter than her sister would have been but ready to defend her mistress. She gave her one more pat. "It's Uncle Grey," she said as the man himself walked in carrying an overnight bag and, more importantly, a pizza.

She got up to help him, taking the box from his hands and bringing it to the table. "Is Jamie mad at me?"

"Of course not. He knows you wouldn't ask without a good reason." He hugged her and kissed her cheek before heading for the smaller guest bedroom. "Besides, taking a night off keeps the mystery alive," he tossed over his shoulder.

"Ha! Mystery is the last thing I need. I'm up to my eyeballs in mystery these days." She walked into the kitchen to grab plates and napkins. "Beer or soda?"

"I'm about to hear something I don't want to. What do you think?"

"Beer, it is."

They settled at her tiny kitchen table, Lily sitting in-between them, smart dog that she was. Grey leaned down and rubbed her head. "Waiting for a taste of crust?"

She cocked her head at his words, her plume of a tail sweeping the hardwood floor.

He finished off a whole piece without saying a word to her. "Okay, I'm ready. Tell me what happened."

Her favorite pizza turned to dust in her mouth. "I think someone tried to kill me tonight."

Chapter Nine

If not for the seriousness of the subject, she would have laughed as Grey's blue eyes widened.

"Not again," he muttered. "I thought we were done with all that." Those same eyes narrowed. "Is there something you forgot to mention? Like maybe some dreams you had, young lady?"

She ducked her head, never able to lie to him. "I only had one. And it didn't mean anything." She cleared her throat. "At least until Gwen, uh, died."

"You mean until someone murdered Gwen. And even having one is something you should have told me." He slid her chair closer to his. "Spill."

"It started like last time, sort of. Vague, all dark and scary without any information. Except I only had one." She took a swig of his beer. "The night before Gwen died." She told him about being in the dark room. "Now, I know it was the back room at Dyeing for Change."

He held her hand. "Oh, honey."

She told him about the park, and the men on the motorbike. Tears spilled as she told him about Gracey.

He handed her a paper napkin. "But she's going to be okay, right?"

The wobble in his voice almost unraveled her. Grey loved the girls almost as much as she did. "Yes, she will be. I feel terrible that she got hurt because of me, though."

He shook his head. An unruly lock of blonde hair fell over one eye. "Oh, no. Gracey is hurt because a mean person did that to her. Not because of you." He brushed the hair away and stared her down. "Say it. This is not your fault."

"This is not my fault," she parroted back to him.

He gave her hand a squeeze. "Good. Now tell me the part about yummy Detective Wolfe."

"Noah is a great catch."

"For someone else. You need zing. You need someone who sets your pulse running." He stopped talking then, staring at her as she felt the warmth spread across her face. "What?"

She relayed the conversation with *Jonah* from earlier in the evening. Funny how she always thought of him by his given name, even though they acted very formal with each other.

One perfect brow arched. "Oh really? Interesting."

"'Interesting'? That's all I get?"

"You know my thoughts on the subject. Noah is very nice, but boring and not for you. Detective Hottie, on the other hand, is so not boring. And you admit to the zing. And now, after trying to remain impartial, he's flirting with you. Must you be hit over the head? Again? Go for it. Jump that man. Invite him to dinner. Or breakfast. For the love of all that's holy, do something." He sat back, took a sip of his beer and winked at her.

"You might have a point. Life is short. And unpredictable."

"Hallelujah! Shave your legs, put on a short, frilly skirt. Then again, he's seen you covered in blood. It probably doesn't matter what you wear."

"I'd prefer to get my life together before I take this leap. You know, not have someone trying to kill me."

He waved a hand in the air. "Details."

"I really don't want to tell him that the dreams have started again. He already thinks I'm weird. Let's not add to it."

"He doesn't think you're weird, per se."

"You're splitting hairs."

"All I'm saying is that he knows about the dreams and the mysterious protector or whatever, and he hasn't run for the hills."

"Thanks a lot."

"But it's true. Think of it this way. You know how when you meet someone new and it's like a honeymoon period? They haven't learned all your little idiosyncrasies yet."

"Has Jamie discovered your ridiculous need to remove clothing from the dryer the second the buzzer sounds?"

"Hey! No one likes wrinkles. At least I don't leave it in the washer until I have to wash it again. Eww. Just saying."

"Once! I did that once, maybe five years ago. Let it go, Princess. And what about you? God forbid anything in your fridge is even an hour out of date."

"It happened more than once. And that's just being healthy. Who wants to eat expired food?"

"It's a 'best if served by' date. You won't die of food poisoning if you eat something the day after it expires."

"You have cottage cheese older than Lily. And you don't eat cottage cheese."

"But I should. It's good for you." A laugh bubbled up from within her, spilling out until the sound filled the room.

Grey joined in until he doubled over, gasping for breath. He waved a hand in the air. "Stop. Must breathe," he gasped.

The doorbell rang. Lily ran to the door, staring at it, then at Addie over her shoulder.

She grabbed a napkin and dabbed her eyes. "Whew, I really needed that." She wrapped her arms around her ribs, cradling them. "I can't remember the last time I laughed like that." She walked to the door, peeking through the peep hole. And her heart skipped a beat. Or two hundred.

She opened the door. "Detective Wolfe. I didn't expect to see you again tonight." She took a step back. "Come in." She closed the door behind him before leading the way to the kitchen.

He glanced at the pizza box. "I'm sorry. I didn't mean to disturb your dinner." He inclined his head at Grey. "Mr. Waverly, good evening. I'm glad to see you're staying here tonight."

"Tell me, Detective Wolfe. What is your worst habit?"

"Grey!" She turned to the detective. "Feel free to ignore him. I do. Would you like some pizza?"

"Oh, I don't want to intrude," he exclaimed as his stomach rumbled.

Addie laughed. "It's no bother. Let me get a plate."

"You'd better warn him first," Grey called.

"Warn me?"

She handed him a plate. "Oh, he means about the pizza. There's pineapple on it." She waited for his look of scorn. Not everyone got it.

But he opened the box and picked up a slice. He took a big bite, chewed and swallowed.

She tried to not drool watching.

Grey stared at him. "You like pineapple on your pizza?"

"Yes, don't you?"

"Only after years of conditioning." He jerked a thumb in her direction. Grey leaned forward, resting his chin in his hand. "Tell me. What's the oldest thing in your fridge?"

"Grey! Stop it!" She turned to the detective. "Don't mind him. He's off his meds."

Detective Wolfe turned his head, looking from one to the other. "Did I miss something?"

She counted to ten in her head. "We were listing each other's faults before you arrived. Don't feel obligated to answer."

"Are you sure you two aren't married?"

"Oh, we're not. But we may have a child together soon." With that bombshell, Grey stood. "I'm going to go check in with Jamie. See if he misses me." He smirked at Addie and left the room.

She busied her hands, grabbing another slice of pizza. And waited for the earth to open and swallow her whole. When it didn't, she turned to him. "So, is there something I could help you with?"

He glanced at her mostly flat abdomen. "So, you're not. Uh." He concentrated on his pizza.

"Pregnant? No, I'm not. But thanks for asking. Geesh, I really have to think about joining a gym."

"I didn't mean to imply that you look, uh." He cleared his throat. "I'm going to stop talking now."

She laughed. She couldn't help it. He so rarely squirmed. "Grey referred to a pact we made when we were, like, nineteen."

"To have a baby together? Even though he's…"

"Gay? Yes, I know it sounds ridiculous. But we were young and tipsy one night. So, we swore if we were both single at thirty-five, we'd have a baby together." She sighed. "Back then, thirty-five seemed like a lifetime away. Not so much anymore."

"There's always Dr. Barrett. Maybe he wants kids."

"I'm sure you didn't come back to discuss him." She squelched a wince at her tone. Bitchy bordering on fishwife.

He stared for a second before his expression closed. "You're right." He pulled his phone from his pocket and swiped across the screen. "This is a photo I took of an email I received tonight." He turned the phone so she could see.

She read the words 'Watch over her'. "What does that mean?"

"I got this at work today. My tech guy is trying to trace it now. I thought you should know."

And you couldn't have called? She kept that thought to herself. "I'm assuming it's my mysterious protector, back again."

"Seems that way. I hoped you might have come up with something."

She paced the length of the tiny kitchen. "I have been over this again and again. Nothing. Who could it be? None of this makes any sense."

"I didn't mean to upset you."

"How would this not upset me? Some person, a stranger, feels the need to protect me. From a distance this time. I have no idea who he is or why he feels this need. It feels creepy, almost like he's stalking me. And yet, he saved me. More than once."

He stepped in front of her, stopping her pacing. His dark eyes brimmed with something she couldn't identify. "Don't get me wrong. I'm glad for that. But I'd feel better if I knew who it is."

"You and me both. But if your tech guy can't trace the email, what do we do?"

He dragged a hand through his short dark hair. She watched, clenching her own hands into fists to stop from doing the same. She itched to touch him. Hold his hand. Wrap her arms around his waist and lay her cheek against his chest. Do all kinds of things she shouldn't be thinking about.

"Ms. Foster?"

She started. Pulled herself from that train of thought. "Yes?"

"Where were you?"

"Oh." She felt the warmth creep across her cheekbones. "I, uh. Never mind. What do we do next?"

He didn't answer right away, just watched her as if searching her thoughts. She hoped not. "Hopefully, the flash drive will turn up something. In the meantime, you need to be very careful. Don't take any chances. Don't go anywhere alone. And for God's sake, don't go back to the park. In fact, don't leave your house." He muttered something else she couldn't quite catch.

"Are you kidding me? I didn't do anything wrong. And in case you forgot, I have a business to run. I am not going to sit in my house and twiddle my thumbs."

"I need you to be safe. Can you understand that?"

His low, rough tone sent a rush of warmth through her. She reached out, placing a hand on his arm. Even through his jacket and shirt, heat radiated to her palm. And shot bolts of electricity up her arms and throughout her body.

"I can. Really. But I can't just interrupt my life. I'll be careful." She used the other hand to cross her heart. "I promise."

"I believe you. But things have a way of happening to you." His dark eyes blazed as he stared into hers. All the air in the room seemed to disappear. She leaned into him, him into her, until mere inches separated them.

"So, kids, what did I miss?"

Chapter Ten

Addie sprang back, lips pressed in a tight line. Lips that had been seconds away from touching his. "We were discussing Gwen's murder, if you must know." She turned away from the detective and glared at Grey. Her mother used that same look on her when she misbehaved as a child. Called it the 'stop mud in midair look'. He smirked in return. It never worked on him.

"Is that what the kids are calling it these days? Because from where I stood, it looked like y'all were set to smooch. Course, I could be wrong, being gay and all. Maybe you straight folks do it differently." And with that, he sauntered to the fridge and helped himself to a beer. He held aloft a cold IPA from their favorite local brewery, Makai, in Ocean Isle Beach.

She grabbed it from his hand. "I'll take one of those." She twisted off the cap and tipped back her head, drinking half of it in a single go. "Mind your manners, Grey."

He shrugged before grabbing another for himself. "Oh, did you want one, Detective Wolfe?"

"No, thank you. I'm on duty."

Grey arched an eyebrow before glancing at the microwave clock. "Still? Don't you ever get a break?"

"I might if your less than cooperative BFF wouldn't be so stubborn. Then I could focus on this murder and not on worrying about her."

"You didn't really suggest that to her, did you?" He winced at the other man's nod. "Wow, you seemed like a smart man. How'd that go?"

"Not too well."

"I'm right here, by the way. I can hear you." She resisted the urge to stomp one bare foot.

"She hates to be the center of attention." He struck a pose. "That's usually my job."

"I hate being spoken to as though I were a small child. Or brain damaged," she ground out between clenched jaws.

"Did you notice she has a temper?"

"Grey!"

"I'm beginning to get that."

She whirled on the detective. "Not you too." Addie grabbed her plate, no longer hungry. She tossed a scrap of crust to the ever-thankful Lily, who caught it mid-air. "Good girl," she murmured. She rinsed her plate and placed it in the dishwasher. Better to keep her hands busy to avoid strangling her BFF. She counted to thirty in her head before turning around.

"As we discussed, I have a business to run. One which requires me to be there. But as I am neither stupid nor suicidal, I will agree to not take chances."

"Well, that's a relief," Detective Wolfe noted.

She watched from the corner of her eye as Grey leaned back against the counter and folded his arms. A snort escaped him. "I promise to not dash out anywhere alone. Grey can be my babysitter."

"Be careful and smart. Don't go anywhere alone. Don't take any unnecessary chances."

She narrowed her eyes at him. "Really? That's not what you were demanding a few minutes ago."

He glanced at Grey, who laughed and shrugged his shoulders. "You're on your own."

"I know you want to find out who killed your friend. Believe me, so do I. But it's my job, not yours. Go about your life. Go to work. Just don't do anything foolish." He took a step closer forcing her to look at him. "Please."

Then he rinsed his plate before putting it in the dishwasher. "I have to go. Grey, I'm counting on you."

Grey straightened up, approached the detective. "You have my word," he replied, offering his hand. The two shook on it. Then Detective Wolfe gave her one last, lingering look, patted Lily's head, and left.

"Wow, I'm so sorry. I didn't know he was about to kiss you. I would have stayed in the guest room. Or at least waited a few minutes."

"Very funny. I have no business kissing him when I'm dating Noah." She slapped a hand to her forehead. "Oh no. I should have called him tonight. Let him know how I am."

"You mean you haven't checked in with the hubby?"

She let that one go, rubbing her temples instead. Picking up her phone, she dashed him a very bland, watered down version of events and hit send before she could overthink it. "There. He knows I'm home and safe. That's all he needs to know."

Grey pushed off the counter and wrapped her in his arms. "You know I'm only joking. He's not the man for you, and we both know it. Even Detective Hottie knows it. Noah is the only one who doesn't. Let him go. Before you hurt him."

She nodded against his chest. "Yep." Then she took a step back. "But it doesn't seem fair. He's a nice, good looking, doctor for heaven's sake. Even the Aunties like him."

"First of all, the Aunties are desperate for the next generation. So, anything in pants will do. Besides that, you can't force these things. You're not attracted to him, and that's not going to change. And you are way too young to settle." He smirked. "And then there's the thing with the dog hair."

"Right? He isn't a dog person. I can't love a man who worries about getting dog hair on his clothes."

"There you go. Decision made. Now all you have to do is break it to him." He stretched his arms over his head. "It's been a long day. I'll take Lily for one last walk. You straighten up and take a nice, hot shower. And call the clinic to check on Gracey. You'll sleep better." He kissed her cheek and whistled for Lily.

She stood there, watching her best friend take her little dog for a walk, talking to her all the way out the door. Not even for the millionth time, she thanked the universe for giving her such a person. She made a quick call and discovered that Gracey was resting comfortably. Then she cleaned up the kitchen and put the pizza box in the fridge.

A few minutes later, she stood under the strong, hot spray in her shower, washing away the tension of the day. Her heart ached for Gracey, lying in a cage at the vet. But all in all, things could have been so much worse. Gracey would come home soon.

But the hot spray couldn't turn off her thoughts. Or ease the acid in her stomach. Someone had killed Gwen in cold blood. Why? Would the flash drive contain anything? The people after it couldn't know she didn't have it anymore. Would they come after her again?

She stood there until the water turned chilly before turning it off and getting out. She wrapped herself in an oversized towel, comforted by the sounds of Grey moving around in her house. She'd always liked living alone and loved her little house. Until this summer and an unfortunate series of events.

After drying off and throwing on PJs, Addie went out to join Grey. An ecstatic Lily pounced on her the second she came into view. She picked her up and carried her to the couch.

Grey walked out of the guest room, similarly attired, yawning. "So, what's the plan for tomorrow?"

"Life goes back to normal. We go to work. Detective Wolfe solves the murder." The smile slid from her face. "Oh, and I break up with Noah."

"Sounds like a plan." He crossed the room to scratch Lily behind the ears. "Well then, I'm off to sleep."

"You mean after a little phone sex with Jamie."

"Well, of course." He grinned before leaning down to kiss the top of her head. "Don't be a hater. I'm sure Detective Hottie could help you out with that. After you end things with Noah, of course. Goodnight."

Lily whined, watching him leave the room. "I know you love your Uncle Grey. And you miss your sister. It's been a tough day all around. Let's go to bed."

Lily hopped to the floor and ran to her bedroom door, looking over her shoulder as if trying to hurry her along.

"I'm coming," she told the dog. But first she checked all the doors, making sure they were locked. Then she set the alarm. Feeling safer, she followed Lily. After brushing her teeth, she slid into bed, exhaustion settling deep into her bones.

She patted the bed next to her. Lily looked up from the dog bed she usually shared with Gracey, head tilted. "It's okay, girl.

Come sleep with Mommy." Being a smart dog, Lily didn't need another invitation and jumped up. Turning in place, she settled at the foot of the bed and closed her eyes.

Addie settled in as well, hoping for sleep to take her sway from this miserable day. But a few hours later, she lay on her back, eyes wide open, staring at the ceiling fan. Even though Grey slept down the hall, every creak made her jump. Every shadow from the moonlight sent shivers down her spine.

She got up, hoping something from the kitchen might help. Not bothering with a robe, she padded silently out to the kitchen, with Lily glued to her side. She wasn't one to pass up the possibility of a midnight snack. But she passed the kitchen and continued to the front door. Pulling aside the privacy panel on the window, she peeked out into the darkness. Sure enough, a dark sedan sat under the trees across the street. A different feeling overcame her.

She slid the curtain back into place and stood there, thinking about Detective Wolfe. Once again, he had forsaken his own comfort to ensure her safety. A warmth settled in her chest. But she couldn't have him sleeping in his car again. Not when she owned a perfectly comfortable couch.

She ran back in her room and added a light sweatshirt over the shorts and tank she slept in. She headed to the linen closet, grabbing a pillow and sheets. Then she picked up her phone and sent him a text.

"You can't sleep in your car again. The door will be unlocked in fifteen seconds."

She hurried to turn off the alarm. Then she threw the pillow and linen on the couch. She unlocked the door and opened it. He moved with the grace of a jungle cat, all long limbs and controlled gait. Their eyes met, and she stepped back to allow him to enter. No one spoke until she closed and locked the door.

Lily, happy to have her new friend back, leaned up against his leg when he reached down to pet her. The swing of her tail showed her delight. He always knew exactly where she liked to be scratched.

"Why are you up so late?" he asked in that bedroom voice of his. "And where's your watchdog?"

"Can't turn off my mind. And as for watchdogs, she's right here, hoping for a late-night snack."

One corner of his mouth lifted. "I meant Grey."

"I know. But he's hopeless. Could sleep through a bomb, that one." She jerked her thumb at the closed guest room door. "He's been out cold for hours."

"Not much help."

"He has a black belt." She smiled at his widened eyes. "He's tougher than he looks. But he'd have to wake up first."

"Good to know." His eyes never left hers.

She noticed he had changed into jeans and a light windbreaker. The bulge at his hip meant he was armed. She glanced at the couch next to them, suddenly shy in the dim room. "So, there's a pillow and some sheets. If you'd like a blanket, I could get you one."

"I have everything I need, thanks." He turned away, stripping off his jacket as he did. The cotton T-shirt underneath emphasized the muscles of his back and upper arms. Not to mention brought a little drool to the corners of her mouth.

"Okay then. I'm going to grab a snack from the kitchen before I head back to bed."

At the mention of snack, Lily ran to her side.

"This one is very motivated by food. See you in the morning."

"Goodnight, Ms. Foster."

"Goodnight, Detective Foster." *Goodnight, Jonah.*

She turned and headed to the kitchen. And tried to not think about the fact that he would be asleep on her couch, just steps away from her. *How would she ever sleep now?* Ignoring the impulse to join him, she reached for the fridge door instead. When in doubt, eat your emotions. She'd learned that from The Aunties. And every female she'd ever known.

Knowing she would regret it, Addie reached for the pizza box. Cold pizza really should be another food group. Not bothering with a plate, she grabbed a paper towel and sat at the table. Lily, who didn't discriminate against cold pizza crust either, sat at her feet.

A moment later, she felt rather than saw him join her in the darkened kitchen. Felt it in the quickening of her breath, the racing of her heart. "There's a few pieces left," she said by way of invitation.

"Don't mind if I do." He sat across from her before reaching for a slice.

"I used to sleep like it was an Olympic sport. No bad dreams. No racing thoughts. No lying awake for hours." She sighed. "I really miss those days."

"I know the feeling. This job isn't really one you can leave at the office."

"I can imagine." She put down her pizza slice and wiped her mouth. "You have a tough job. One that most wouldn't want. But you're making a difference, Detective Wolfe. I thought you should know."

He stared at her for so long that she wasn't sure she had said the right thing. But then he responded. "Thank you. That means a lot. Some days are tougher than others. Some days, I'm not so sure."

"Did you always want to be a cop?"

He swallowed hard. "Ever since September 2, 1988."

The tiny hairs on her arms stood erect. But she had to ask. "What happened?"

He grew silent again, but a host of emotions flashed across his face. When he finally spoke, it came out as a whisper. "I was helping my dad at the small grocery he owned in Atlanta. The temperature soared that day. I didn't want to be there. I wanted to go swimming with my friends." He stopped for a moment, took a bite of his pizza. "I decided to give him the silent treatment. And then a man came in. He wasn't acting right. Kind of nervous. Talked a mile a minute. Found out later he was high as a kite."

"Later?" Her heart pounded in her chest.

"After he shot my dad. Apparently, he didn't empty the register fast enough." He stared through her, his eyes unfocused. "Right before that happened, my dad signaled me to be quiet. I'd been in the back, sweeping an aisle. I hid behind a display of canned vegetables, my eyes squeezed shut. The gunshot sounded like a cannon."

She reached across the table, taking his icy hand in her warm ones. "You couldn't have done anything. What were you, maybe ten?"

"Eight. It seemed to happen in slow motion, but really it ended in seconds. He took the money and then shot him. Like an after-thought. That's when I screamed. I jumped, and cans flew everywhere. My dad must have hit the silent alarm. A cop came in, gun drawn, just as the man raised his gun to shoot me. 'Can't leave any witnesses,' he told me, still smiling when the cop shot him dead in his tracks. Then he sat with me while we waited for paramedics who couldn't do anything to save my dad."

He still wore that faraway look. So, Addie took the seat next to him. "Oh, Jonah, you couldn't have saved him. I'm so sorry."

He turned his head, and the ghost of a smile appeared on his lips. "Say it again. I like it when you say my first name."

"Jonah," she whispered before laying her head on his shoulder. They sat that way for a while, her heartbeat ticking away the moments. His hand gripped hers as though she had become his lifeline.

"That cop, Officer James Bowden, saved my life that day. He also gave me purpose, direction. From that moment on, I wanted to be like him. Become a cop."

"And you did. I'm sure he's proud of you."

"He is. Was. I lost him to lung cancer a few years ago."

"Oh." She squeezed his hand. "I can't imagine how horrible that must have been for you. I lost my mom young, as you know, but not like that."

"My mom was so lost. But she had my sisters and I to think about. She sold the store. Couldn't be there after what happened. We moved out of the city to be nearer to her family. And to be safer, I guess. Not that anywhere is safe."

"I used to think that Ocean Grove was safe. I wasn't naïve, mind you. I always locked my car and house doors. But how many people don't give it a second thought?"

"Too many." His breath tickled her forehead as he spoke. "Think you can sleep now?"

Was he kidding? "I hope so." But she didn't move. Sitting here, in the dark with him, brought them closer than ever. She really needed to have that talk with Noah.

"It's getting late. I hope to have something from my tech guy in the morning." He chuckled, the vibration of it going right through her. "It's not like on TV. We have to wait for results."

She sat up, turning her head towards him. He was *that* close. So, she moved, putting the table between them. "I hope he gives you something you can use. I need this to end."

He stood. "Agreed." He took a step or two closer, then stopped. "When this is over, all over, I'd like things to be different between us."

She nodded. "Goodnight." She turned and fled the kitchen. *While she still could.* Back in her room, she closed the door and leaned against it. He lay right out there. Would be sleeping on her couch. And suddenly, she knew she could sleep. Despite all that. She brushed her teeth again and climbed back into bed. Lily joined her without waiting to be invited.

And the second her head hit the pillow, Addie fell fast asleep.

Chapter Eleven

She raised one foot to the next step, dread sweeping over her. Dim light shone at the top of the staircase. But it didn't ease her mind. Cold sweat ran down her sides and back. Another step up, closer. "Grey, I don't think this is a good idea." He didn't answer her, just nudged her forward from behind. She looked around at the unfamiliar place. Where were they? "I agree," came a disembodied voice from the top.

She woke to the sensation of someone watching her. She opened her eyes to find Lily inches from her face. "Oh, thank goodness. Good morning, Lily. Did your bladder or your tummy wake you?"

She whined in response, jumping off the bed and stood at the door.

"Okay, keep your fur on." Pushing sweat matted hair from her eyes, Addie slid out of bed. She cracked the door and listened. Sure enough, two male voices reached her ears. *Great!* You never knew what would come out of Grey's mouth. She opened the door, allowing Lily out, then closed it behind her. He would know what to do. She didn't want to leave the two guys out there alone for too long, so she splashed some water on her face and skipped the shower.

"Good morning," she called before joining them in the kitchen. Grey glanced over his shoulder at her from the stove. His raised eyebrow said it all. Detective Wolfe sat at the table, reading the morning paper. All in all, it made a strange tableau.

"Hello," he greeted her.

She pressed a hand to her stomach to calm the flight of butterflies. "Anyone for juice?" She turned to the fridge as though these two men sat in her kitchen every morning. No. Big. Deal.

"Yes, please," they answered in unison.

She nodded before grabbing some glasses.

"Do you want your usual, Addie?"

She smiled at Grey. "You know I do." She glanced at the detective. "He makes a mean Western Omelet."

"The key is in the timing. You have to know when to flip and when to fold." His smile said he wasn't just discussing eggs.

Detective Wolfe glanced at both, as if trying to decide if that was code for something else. He turned to her. "Did you sleep okay?"

"I did, thanks. Went right out like a baby after that pizza. And talk." She held his gaze for a moment before pouring three glass of orange juice.

"Until the muffled scream we just heard. I'm betting another nightmare." He turned to the detective. "Any news this morning?"

"Another?"

She sighed and sat at the table. "I've only had two."

"So far," added Grey from the stove.

"Bite your tongue."

"Were you ever going to tell me?"

She closed her eyes on the hint of hurt in his voice. "Yes."

"Really?"

"Shut up, Grey." She opened her eyes. And told him.

"Hmmm." He set down the paper and scrubbed a hand over his face. "I want you to tell me immediately if you have another."

"Told you he wouldn't think you're a freak."

She turned to Detective Wolfe. "You were about to tell us what you've learned."

"I would never think you were a freak."

And she melted on the spot.

"As for the other, I'm waiting to hear from my tech guy. Sam's a genius with this stuff."

"It'd be nice to get back to normal," she muttered into her juice glass.

"Speaking of 'getting back to normal', when's your lunch date with the good doctor?" Grey slid half of an omelet on the plate in front of the detective. "She's ending it with him today. Hope she doesn't break his heart." He served hers next, with a wink.

"Grey!" She slid a napkin on her lap. And tried to ignore the color she felt spreading across her cheeks. "We went on five dates. He will not be heartbroken."

"Five, huh?" Detective Wolfe asked around a mouthful of eggs. He swallowed before asking, "Isn't three the magic number?"

"If you don't mind, my private life is just that."

His face shuttered at her words. She looked away, wishing she could take them back.

"No worries, Ms. Foster. Wouldn't want to overstep my bounds."

How were they back to this? "I, uh, just meant. Oh, never mind."

Grey sat down at his usual place. He picked up a fork full of eggs and ate them. "Yummy, as always." He turned to the detective. "She's breaking up with him because life is too short to be involved with someone without any zings. And because she can't kiss you until she does. Could you pass the ketchup, please?"

Addie concentrated on swallowing her eggs rather than choking.

He did so, staring at her the whole time. "Is that true?"

"Yes." She never liked games. Something intense swirled between them.

He smiled then. A real smile that reached his eyes and stole her breath. "Okay, then." And then he went back to eating his breakfast.

"Okay," she parroted before eating hers.

Grey laughed. "You two are impossible."

Small talk reigned after that. As he took his last bite, Detective Wolfe's phone alerted to an incoming text. After reading it, he pushed back from the table. "Sam has something interesting. I have to go." He stood and held her gaze for a long moment. "Good luck with lunch." Then he turned to Grey. "Thanks for the best omelet I've ever eaten."

"Of course. I'm never modest about my cooking. And you're welcome."

He barely made it out the door when Grey's head whipped around. "He *really* likes you." He searched her face. "And if I'm not mistaken, and I rarely am, you like him too."

"I do. We sat here and talked last night. In the dark. He told me about losing his dad in a robbery gone wrong. Jonah was eight."

"'Jonah'? Interesting."

"Anyway, I have a lot to do today. Have to get ready for work. Have to figure out who killed Gwen and why."

"Have to break up with Noah over a salad."

"Oh, yeah, that too. Like I said, lots to do."

"And that middle one, about solving her murder, uh uh." He shook his finger at her. "Leave that to the professionals."

"Fine. But I really have to get going."

"I already showered, so I'm going to head in after I clean up."

"Great! I'll be right behind you. But since you're going first, you can stop for coffee." She blew him a kiss and left the room at a run.

"Nice," he yelled down the hall.

*****

Less than an hour later, she entered Smiling Dog Books. Once inside the door, she let Lily off her leash. The dog ran behind the counter. Addie followed a bit slower, stopping to chat with a few customers.

After giving the dog some water and her breakfast, she booted up her laptop. She tapped her nails as she waited for it to warm up, dreading lunch with Noah. Grey had been spot on. The nice doctor seemed way more invested in this relationship than her. He'd texted her three times already this morning about places to eat. Poor man had no idea what was coming. Oh well, better now than later.

"Figured out what you're going to say to Noah?" Grey leaned against the counter as though he didn't have a care in the world.

"No. I have to put the blame on me, not him. Keep it casual." She gnawed her lower lip.

"He's going to be hurt no matter what you say. Devastated, even."

"Thanks. Remind me again why you're my BFF?" She stuck out her tongue at him. "And he'll be just fine. It's only been five dates."

"Ooh, isn't three the magic number?" asked Mrs. Henry, who had to be pushing eighty. She held a romance novel with a half-naked man on the cover. "I'd like to buy this please."

"Of course, Mrs. Henry." She took the book from her to scan and kept her face blank. Mrs. Henry loved her romance novels.

"We aren't talking about that nice Dr. Barrett, are we?" She looked at Addie over the top of her glasses. "He's a cutie patootie, as you young folks say these days. And you're not getting any younger, dear."

"Which of us is?" muttered Grey. "But they didn't have any zing. What can she do?"

"Oh, well that's different. Can't waste your time if there's no zing. That's what I tell the lovely widower down the hall, Bill Hamilton. Always up in my grill, that one. Nice guy but no zing. Not like my Jimmy, God rest his soul. Now, we had zing. More than forty years' worth." She handed over a twenty.

"Hard to beat that, Mrs. Henry," she commented, handing back the older woman's change. She placed the book in her reusable shopping bag. "Enjoy the reading. Come again."

"Thank you. And try not to break his heart, dear." She shook her head on the way out. "Such a shame."

"How does everyone know about the third date rule?"

"It's a thing. Although I'm more of a slut than you. I took Jamie home the first night."

"Well, Noah has barely kissed me. Not sure what that says about me."

"It's more about what it says about him. You're fine. Just dump him already."

"I will. At lunch. And I'm not dumping him, just letting him go."

"Whatever. He's into you. It's not going to end well."

"Please stop saying that. My life is already a mess." She rubbed her temples.

"Is he picking you up here?"

"Ha! I know better. I'm meeting him at the square. Not sure where we're going."

"But Detective Wolfe seemed clear on this. You aren't to be alone."

"Tough. He's not the boss of me, and neither are you."

"But we both care about you and your safety. At least let me walk you there."

She shook her head. "I'll be fine."

"Noah doesn't know, does he?"

"Since he won't be part of my life anymore, there didn't seem much point."

Grey came around the counter and handed her a bag from under it. "Here. At least take this."

She pulled out a new can of mace. And hugged him. "Oh, Grey, how can I ever top this for your birthday?"

"Funny. But seeing how you used the last can, last night, I might add, it seemed appropriate."

"True." She tucked it in her purse. "Okay, I'm off to the back to get some dreaded paperwork done. Hold down the fort." She whistled for Lily and walked away.

Once in her office, she sat in her chair, staring at the wall. She'd feel better after lunch. When she ended it. She hated doing this to Noah. Lily sat at her feet and leaned against her leg in sympathy. She scratched behind her ears. "You're a good girl. Mommy isn't a monster. But she does have to hurt Noah." She sighed and reached for a stack of unopened mail. Dealing with anything other than books and customers tended to give her hives. Or make her sleepy. But that was the fun of owning your own business.

*****

"Are you avoiding breaking his heart?" Grey asked from his position, propped in the doorway.

"What?" She glanced at the clock on her computer screen. "How is it almost twelve? Why didn't you come find me sooner?" She jumped up, fluffing her hair. "I have to go. At least I got some work done." She grabbed her purse. "Can you watch Lily for me? I may be right back."

Grey put an arm around her shoulder. "You're doing the right thing. It'll be okay, Noah is a big boy."

"I know."

"Come on. Use the Band-Aid method."

"What?"

"You know. Just pull quickly."

"Gee, thanks."

"Remember the zing, or the lack thereof. And remember Heathcliff."

"We can't keep calling him that. We might slip up and do it in front of Detective Wolfe." She grinned. "He does so remind me of the character though." *Swoon.*

"All right, enough daydreaming. Go break his heart."

"I have my mace, I'm ready."

His laughter followed her out the door.

Chapter Twelve

"It's because I'm not a dog person, isn't it?"

Addie cringed at Noah's accusation. Or maybe at the strange looks of the other fifteen or so patrons in their section of the restaurant. She plastered a smile on her face and glanced around the elegant restaurant to see if people heard. Then turned back to him. "No, it's not that." *He doesn't like dogs?* She shook off that thought.

"Then is it because we've gone out five times and haven't had sex?"

The fake smile slipped. "Noah," she hissed. "Please lower your voice." No glancing around this time. No way they missed that nugget. She took a sip of iced water. They hadn't even ordered yet. Her stomach rumbled. Her head pounded. This was not going well. Damn Grey for always being right. She started to reach a hand toward him but stopped. No use sending mixed signals.

"Is there a problem here?"

Her appetite vanished at the voice. Of course! Back on went the fake smile. "Hello, Tiffany. Noah and I just need another second to order. Don't we?" Tiffany Blackwell, back to her maiden name after not one but two failed marriages, owned the restaurant. And the place of honor in all of Addie's high school nightmares. Petite and blonde, although only after third grade, Tiffany Blackwell was the spoiled only child of the Ocean Grove Blackwells. They had money and made sure everyone knew. Addie Foster, an orphan with no claim to fame, wouldn't normally even reach their radar. Except that Tiffany only felt better about herself when she made others feel worse about themselves. And she never let her do that. Thus, mortal enemies.

"So, you'll need more time?" She directed her acidic tone to Addie, while Noah received her best, teeth-whitened smile. "This is our busiest time of the day, you know."

"Thank you, Tiffany," she muttered.

"That won't be necessary." Noah stood, placing his napkin on the chair. "Apparently, not only am I not good enough for her, she refuses to even tell me why." He stalked off, leaving her with Tiffany.

Great! Could this get any worse?

"You left him?" Tiffany's voice hit a pitch that threatened everything made of glass.

Apparently, it could. She rose, placing her napkin on the table. Rummaging through her bag, Addie threw a five on the table for the waitress's trouble. "Guess we won't be ordering after all."

She left without making any eye contact and never slowed until she'd walked a block. She sat on a bench in the shade of a maple tree. Breathe in. Breathe out. Her stomach rumbled once again. She'd never been one of those women who couldn't eat when upset. Damn. She closed her eyes and tried to untangle what had just happened when she heard a car approach the curb in front of her. Remembering the fact that she had been attacked twice yesterday, her eyes flew open. And there sat Jonah in his unmarked police car. She almost would have preferred the other. At least she could have used her brand-new mace. Her shoulders slumped as she watched him exit the car and approach her. He sat at the other end of the bench.

"What part of not going anywhere alone didn't you get?"

She turned to him, wanting to stroke that jaw that resembled granite. She folded her hands in her lap instead. "I couldn't very well bring Grey to lunch with Noah, now could I?" She reached in her purse and pulled out the gift. "He did give me this, though." A high-pitched laugh escaped her.

His face softened. "It didn't go well, huh? You laugh when you're nervous."

"Oh. You remembered."

"There's not a lot I've forgotten about you, Ms. Foster."

And a different emotion replaced the hunger in her belly. "No, it didn't go well. Not to mention the fact that the usually soft-spoken Noah suddenly developed an outside voice, inside, and my childhood nemesis got to watch. All in all, I'd call it a complete disaster." And to add to her humiliation, her stomach rumbled. "And I didn't even get to eat."

"Why don't I give you a ride back to the store, with a stop for food. Maybe mac and cheese? Or ice cream?"

She gaped at him. "Doesn't sound like your normal lunch choices, Detective Wolfe."

"Nope, but they are comfort foods. I have sisters, remember?"

"Definitely ice cream, then. It's too hot for mac and cheese. Besides, I only eat Henri's, and I've already met my quota for the week."

"I didn't know Henri made mac and cheese."

"Only for me. But he insists I call it macaroni au fromage. Otherwise, it's beneath him."

He stood, offering her a hand. "Udderly Delicious it is, then."

At the mention of her favorite ice cream on the planet, she placed her hand in his, tried to ignore the zings, and stood. She looked up into his eyes. A slight smile curled her lips. "Consider yourself warned. It's an Everything but the Kitchen Sink kind of day."

His eyes rounded. "That bad, huh? I think I can handle it." He nodded his head towards the car. "Shall we?"

"Lead the way."

He dropped her hand and opened her door, closing it once she got in. Then he walked around the hood and got in.

She looked around the interior. "I've never been in a police car. Unless you count at an open house as a child."

"That's good to know." He pulled out into traffic, keeping up a stream of small talk that shocked her. She always thought of him as quiet, maybe even reserved.

He pulled into the place, across the street from the beach, and lowered their windows. Rivaling their cute name was the fact that the wait staff wore roller blades. Within a minute, a high schooler rolled up, asking for their order.

"The lady will have the Everything but the Kitchen Sink. I'll have a hot dog, Coke, and fries, please."

The young girl scowled at him. Then leaned in to look at Addie. "What did he do to you?"

"Excuse me?" the detective asked.

Addie giggled. "Oh, it wasn't him. He's just putting me out of my misery by feeding me ice cream."

"Oh." She turned to him. "Sorry, dude. I'll be right back with your orders."

She pressed her hand against her mouth to prevent any more giggles escaping. "Did Sam have anything for you?"

He turned to her. "I, um, can't really tell you. Ongoing investigation and all that." He had the grace to at least look uncomfortable.

"Oh, that's disappointing. Can you at least tell me if Diana was her real name?"

His lips pressed into a flat line. "Fine. Gwen's real name was Diana Campanella. She was forty-two and lived in New York City. Happy?"

"No, not really. I thought that Gwen and I were friends. But I didn't even know her real name."

His mouth softened. "There's a very good reason for that. And it had nothing to do with you."

"Witness Protection."

He raised one dark brow, the one with the scar. "That wasn't a question."

"No. What other reason is there for changing her whole identity? Moving hundreds of miles away? And never speaking about her past? She couldn't change that accent though."

"You may have missed your calling."

She shook her head. "No. I love books and being surrounded by them all day. Not to mention hating the stress that yours brings." She pulled at the waistband of her capris. "These aren't going to fit soon if this keeps up."

His gaze travelled the length of her. "I don't think you have anything to worry about."

She returned his look, taking her own bold survey of his frame.

"Here you go," announced the girl on blades.

The moment evaporated.

He turned to the window, taking Addie's ridiculously large sundae and handing it to her. "Good luck with that."

She laughed at his look of skepticism. "I wasn't planning on finishing it. And I might even share. If asked properly."

"You're on." He poured ketchup on his hot dog and took a bite. "So, do you want to talk about it?"

She sighed, holding the spoon overloaded with a concoction of ice cream in midair. "Not really. Noah is a nice guy."

"But lacking zing, according to Grey."

"We lacked zing together. It's not all on him."

He wiped his hands on a paper napkin. The he leaned in ever so slightly towards her. And pushed one stray ebony curl behind her ear.

Her breath hitched.

"It was him, not you. Trust me." Then he ate a few fries.

And she remembered to breathe. She took another spoonful. "I never even got to explain. Once he heard, 'We have to talk', it was all over."

He winced. "There's never a good reason to hear those words."

She pushed the spoon around in her sundae, appetite momentarily gone. "I know. I choked. There's no good way to break up with someone. Whatever you say, they get hurt. And you feel badly. But I didn't except him to raise his voice." She looked around the parking lot and lowered her voice. "I didn't want to make a scene."

"So, maybe a public place wasn't the way to go."

"In hindsight, no. But it had to be today."

"Because you want to kiss me. And you wouldn't while you were still seeing him. I like that."

"I still may kill Grey."

That oh so delectable dimple flashed. "But then I'd have to arrest you. And where would that leave us?"

She fiddled with the napkin in her lap. "Is there an us?"

"I'd like there to be." He took a sip of his soda. "And we already have the zing covered."

"And *you* like dogs."

He tilted his head. "He didn't like dogs? How would work with the girls?"

And her chest filled with a rush of warmth. "I didn't figure that out until a few minutes ago. He thought I ended it because of them."

"For the record, I love dogs. I don't have one due to my crazy hours and living alone. But I love them. I have a thing for shaggy little dogs with huge personalities."

"Turns out, so do I."

He eyed her ice cream. "Are you ready to share?"

"I just might be."

Chapter Thirteen

Addie waved goodbye when he dropped her off in front of her store. She raised her face to the sun, delighting in the beautiful day, before entering the store, whistling a happy tune. Lily came out from behind the counter to greet her. She knelt and buried her face in the dog's silky fur. "Oh. Lily, what a wonderful day to be alive." Lily yipped in return.

"So, I'm guessing lunch went better than expected. Tell me everything. I'm all ears."

Her smile slipped the tiniest bit. "No, lunch sucked. He took me to Tiffany's, despite my protests." She shuddered, remembering the look on her old enemy's face.

"Oh, no he didn't. That was the worst possible place to go."

"Tell me about it. And it went downhill from there." She told him every detail about lunch and sat back, waiting for the inevitable explosion. She didn't have to wait long.

"Are you kidding me? The nerve of him, blaming this on you. The nerve of that little witch, taking delight in this. Why, I have a mind to..."

She threw her arms up in the air. "Stop right there. If you remember, Noah is the injured party."

The look on Grey's handsome face said otherwise.

"No, he is. I broke up with him. And as Detective Wolfe pointed out, doing so in a public place may not have been the best choice."

"How did Detective Hottie become involved in this? Did you forget to tell me something?"

She groaned and placed her head in her hands. She blamed the ton of ice cream. She told him about how he found her sitting on the bench. "So, he took me for ice cream."

"To Udderly Delicious? And no doggie bag?"

His frown made her laugh. "I could have brought you the rest of the Sink special."

"Oh, Addie, you didn't."

She hung her head. "I did. But he helped. And then he asked me out. Sort of."

"Ah, now we get to the smiling and whistling part. Tell me everything. What does 'sort of' mean?"

"Well, like last time, he's not comfortable dating someone involved in an active investigation. Ethics and all that." She waved a hand.

"So, the faster we get this figured out, the better."

"There's no we in this, Grey. Let's just leave this to the professionals."

He laughed and then stared. "Oh, you were serious. Bummer."

"Gwen's real name was Diana Campanella. And as we thought, Witness Protection placed her here. That's all he'd tell me."

"And you're just going to leave it at that? Note the skepticism in my voice."

She looked away. "Well, I did have a thought about checking out her apartment above the shop. Maybe if we could get in, we'd find something."

"And by we, you mean you and I, right?"

"I don't really want to involve you any further in this. But I need a lookout."

"You're my BFF. I'm already involved."

"How good are you at picking locks?"

*****

Just after dark, they met in the alley behind Dyeing for Change. She tried to not laugh at Grey, dressed all in black like a would-be cat burglar. He even wore a black knit cap pulled low over his blond hair.

"You changed," she called to him as he approached.

"You didn't."

"Not true. I put on jean capris and a baseball cap." She pointed to her Wilmington Sharks hat.

"You're not exactly dressed for breaking into this place."

"You're dressed for Mission Impossible."

"Let's just do this." She walked to the back door of the salon, Grey on her heels. "Remember, you're my lookout."

"Right, Boss. But you have to get in first."

It turned out to be easier than expected. The doorknob turned in her hand. "That's probably not a good sign."

"Well, at least it's just entering now. Not breaking and entering."

"Let's go before I lose my nerve." They entered the back door, pulling it closed behind them. She pointed to a door on the right just inside. "That might lead to her apartment upstairs."

That door stood open a few inches. She pushed it with her toe and crept up the stairs. And right into her nightmare. With each step, the hairs stood up more on the back of her neck. Her blood turned to ice in her veins. She stopped on the last step and turned to him. "This is a very bad idea."

The interior lights flipped on. "I agree," announced a man in a very heavy New York accent. The large gun in his hand froze her in place. He waved it at them, gesturing them forward.

She debated running back down the stairs, for maybe a second. But this wasn't a TV show. The gun was real. And lethal. They killed Gwen, or Diana. They wouldn't hesitate to do it again. She took a few steps into the living room, keeping her back to the wall.

"You too, Mister. And don't try anything funny."

"Oh, I'm very funny," Grey said as he joined her against the wall.

"A wise guy. Great. Just what we need."

"I thought you guys were called that." He turned to Addie. "Isn't the mob referred to as 'wise guys'?"

Another man walked out of what must be the bedroom. "What's going on here?"

She gasped, recognizing him. "You hurt Gracey." Without thinking, she started to approach him. But the gun in the other man's hand stopped her in her tracks.

He turned to his accomplice. "Any chance you forgot to lock the door on the way up?"

"I thought you were going to do that."

"You followed me in. It was your job. Do I have to think of everything?" He sighed. "No matter now. We'll have to dispose of them."

She had to think of something. If she could just get to her phone tucked away in her back pocket.

"Keep an eye on them while I finish looking in Diana's bedroom." He turned and left.

The other man concentrated on them. "Stay right where you are. And don't try anything."

"Or what? You'll shoot us sooner?" She turned to Grey and mouthed, 'Distract him'. She saw his eyes widen and could almost hear the gears in his brain turning.

He took a step towards the goon with the gun. "Did you know that I have a black belt in karate?" he asked. "Why don't you put the gun down to make this a fair fight?" He took another step closer and to the left, blocking the other man's view of her.

She slipped the phone from her pocket and hit the preset for Detective Wolfe. It rang twice before she heard his voice. "Yeah, bringing a gun to a karate fight isn't fair." She slid the phone into the front pocket of her hoodie.

"Or maybe bringing a black belt to a gun fight is stupid." The bigger man laughed.

She hoped Jonah heard all this. "I liked Gwen. I want to know why you killed her downstairs." Now he'd know where they were.

"I'll answer that." The other man returned from the bedroom. "It took me over five years, but I found Diana. Hiding out in this crappy little town. Doing hair, of all things. Did you know her mom worked as a hairdresser? Diana talked about it all the time. How her mom's legs always hurt at the end of a long day. And she came home smelling like chemicals. She hated it. Went to college to be an accountant to avoid living that same life. And look where she ended up."

"Guess she didn't hate it so much, if she chose this for herself."

"Maybe she felt nostalgic. After all, her mother met an untimely end, right after Diana left. Seems there was a short in the wiring of her shop." His grin told her otherwise.

"You still haven't told me why Gwen had to die." They needed time for Jonah to get here. *Please let this work.*

"Diana worked for us, at least for one of our companies. The legal one. She was very smart, did an excellent job. Until she got too nosey. Took too close of a look. She had questions one day, about the other companies behind the shell. The ones that we funneled our profits from other, more profitable ventures through. And she kept proof."

"Oh, you mean the flash drive."

His smirk became a snarl. "You have the flash drive after all?" He took one threatening step towards her. "Where is it?"

"I found it later that night. Gwen, uh Diana, had stashed it in my purse the morning you killed her. You might want to talk to Detective Jonah Wolfe, of the Ocean Grove Police. He has it."

He grabbed her by the upper arm, twisting it. She couldn't stop the yelp of pain that escaped. "You think you're so smart, don't you? So, did Diana. Look where it got her. You two are still going to die. Just like your friend."

"Ah, we weren't friends. I go to the barber shop."

And that was enough to get their attention. Before she knew what happened, Grey's leg flashed out, catching the gunman in his right wrist. The gun flew. Then all Hell broke loose. They scrambled for the fallen gun, while the door burst open below them. The sound of thundering feet on the stairs made her want to cry in relief.

"Freeze!" Several cops, with Jonah in the lead, flooded into the room. There was a lot of confusion and the deafening sound of a single shot.

She turned to Jonah, her knees buckling at the grotesque bloom of crimson across the white T-shirt covering his upper arm. He looked down at the same time, the color seeping from his face.

"No!" she screamed and rushed towards him.

He slid down the wall behind him. Another officer stepped forward, removing the gun from his hand. Addie rushed to his side. "Don't you leave me. I'm right here. I've got you, Jonah." She pressed her hand against his wound, wincing at the blood that seeped through her fingers. "Help!"

Chapter Fourteen

She awoke to the sound of her name. She opened her eyes, lost for a moment. Then she remembered.

"Addie," Jonah whispered, eyes at half-mast.

"Hey, you're back."

"I am. And you're here." His eyes drifted closed.

"Shhh, it's okay. I'll be here when you're awake again." She brushed a thick lock of his hair from his eyes. If you looked past the bandages and machines, he looked younger in his sleep.

She glanced at her phone. Almost three in the morning. And too many missed calls and messages from Grey to count. She dashed off a quick note, letting him know Jonah had made it through surgery. Then she shoved her phone back in her pocket.

The past few hours passed in a blur of questions and worry. Guilt at getting him shot in the first place gnawed at her. Another detective asked many questions of them, not to mention threatening charges for being in Gwen's apartment.

Then there were several hours of pacing and hand wringing. She'd sent Grey to her house to take care of Lily. And to give her some peace. He tended to babble. She shared a waiting room with police officers who didn't know her relationship to their coworker. If they even had one now. She did get him shot.

She rested her head against the railing of his bed. No use worrying about that now. He would make a full recovery. That's all that mattered.

"I can hear you worrying from over here. What's wrong?" he struggled to sit up but then must have thought better of it. "Could I get a sip of water?" he rasped.

She sprang up. "Of course." She poured him a glass from the jug provided and put in a straw. "I'm so very sorry," she murmured and held the straw to his lips. Even in the dim light, his face lacked its normal healthy color.

He took a sip and then laid his head back against the pillows. "Why? Did you shoot me?"

She giggled, curse her nervous habit. "No, of course not. But I'm the reason you got shot."

"No, you're not." He held out his left hand, palm up.

She scooted her chair closer and took his hand in hers. "I thought." She stopped, sniffing back tears. "There was so much blood. Your blood. I thought…"

He raised their joined hands to his mouth, pressing his lips against the back of hers. "I'm right here. I'm fine. And I'm so sorry I scared you." He smiled. "But that makes us even. You took ten right off the top when I figured out where you were. And with whom."

She ducked her head. "Oh, that. Right. Your friend threatened to arrest me. Something about obstruction and breaking and entering. Although, in my defense, we didn't break. The door was open."

He laughed, followed by a wince. "Not a great idea for me right now."

She laid her other hand along his jaw, all bristly with five o'clock shadow. "You rest. There's plenty of time to talk later."

"Now that this case is over, there's plenty of time for us," he whispered, his eyes drifted shut.

The End

Acknowledgments

Thank you to everyone in my life who puts up with what it means to be a writer; the hours of writing, editing, tearing my hair out and writing again. I'm not always fun to live with.

Always to the most patient PA in the world, Margie Greenhow. Where would I be without you??? Although, I will say I have been better this year at staying focused and on track, not forgetting about Facebook takeovers, etc.

For every cover, I have turned to the magic of Rebecca Pau of The Final Wrap. She is so very talented and even more understanding. Each book, I think this is my favorite cover. Then I see the next one. She nailed it once again. Thank you!!

Always to my Mom, no longer with me in person but remains in my heart. She always told me I could do anything I set my mind to. And she was right. Miss you every day.

How to Help an Indie Author

Reviews, reviews, reviews! Even if you don't fall in love with my books, please take the time to review them on Amazon, Goodreads and/or Book Bub. Reviews are so much more important than you could ever imagine.

Stop by my FB page or send me an email. Tell me that you liked my book or why you didn't. Feedback helps.

Follow me everywhere:

Facebook:
https://www.facebook.com/profile.php?id=100012114317732

Twitter:
https://twitter.com/K_OMalley67

Instagram:
https://www.instagram.com/kimberleyomalley67/

Amazon Author Page:
www.amazon.com/author/kimberleyomalley

Good Reads Profile:
http://bit.ly/grKOM

Book Bub profile:
https://www.bookbub.com/profile/kimberley-o-malley

Check out my website at www.kimberleyomalley.com
To keep up with me and my books, sign up for my newsletter:
http://eepurl.com/dgonEX

One more Addie Foster Mysteries book is coming soon. Book 3, Murder by Numbers, releases on February 28th. Here's a sneak peek! Keep in mind, this book is still in the editing process and subject to change.

Excerpt from

Murder by Numbers

Addie Foster lay on her side, hands bound in front of her. Course rope bit into her ankles. An old, musty cloth had been tied around her mouth to ensure her silence. She pulled on the rope surrounding her wrists, hoping for some leeway. No such luck, all her struggle did was tighten the bonds.

The door to the room opened, and she closed her eyes. Better for them to think she was still out from the drug they'd used earlier. They spoke in whispers, as if unsure whether she could hear them. She strained to hear but could only make out their voices, not actual words. The tone, however, was clear. And sent icy shivers down her spine.

The obnoxious blaring of her alarm dragged Addie from the nightmare. She lay in bed, heart pounding. But not only from the dregs of the nightmare that remained. It was more the portent of things to come that bothered her. Ever since suffering a concussion last spring, she'd been prone to weird, often prophetic dreams. *Never could contain lottery numbers though, could they?*

She grabbed her phone to shut off her alarm. Sn then scrolled to her calendar. Estate sale day! Excitement replaced vague worry. Gracey & Lily, her two Shelties, looked up from their bed on the floor. Both yawned and stretched before pouncing on her feet as she swung them out of bed. "Someone didn't have any nightmares, I see. Let's go out!" With those words, the dogs became grey and black streaks, yipping and chasing each other to the kitchen slider. She followed at a slower pace, opening it and releasing them into her fenced back yard. The chilly, morning air nibbled at her bare toes. The stumbled to the fridge.

After pouring herself some juice and promised herself a large coffee on the way, she slid a bagel into the toaster and waited. Her phone came alive with the sound of a shrieking ghost, Grey's idea of Halloween humor.

"Good morning, friend. You're up early for a Saturday. I'm not leaving for over an hour or more." She loved her Saturday adventures into old homes and estates. Grey, not so much. Dragging him at the crack of dawn, as she would have preferred, was out of the question.

"About that."

"Grey, you promised!" Between his significant other, Jamie, and her budding relationship with Jonah, their pal time had taken a hit.

"It's not that I don't want to go traipsing through musty old houses on the off chance of finding a first edition Dickens. And I can hear you rolling your eyes."

She laughed. "You can't hear someone roll their eyes. But I am by the way. Good guess."

"Not a guess. Just over twenty-five years of knowing you. Anyway, as I was saying, I have a reason this time. Erin called me. She's not feeling well. Not sure if it's viral or two much partying on campus last night, but she's not coming in this morning. That leaves me to hold the fort."

Erin Mc Carthy, their not quite full-time help, studied history full time at the University of North Carolina in nearby

Wilmington. "She's not really the partying type. I'll go with something viral."

"Doesn't matter. I'll be here and sadly, not with you."

"You don't have to sound so happy about it."

"I'll miss you, but, no, I won't miss that. You can always take Detective Hottie with you. He has nothing but free time these days."

"Not nice, Grey. Especially since you and I are the reason he got shot." She shuddered remembering those terrifying hours when she wasn't sure how he'd fare.

"My bad. Anyway, maybe he'll go with you."

"Not sure it's his thing."

"He's allowed to defer, and I'm not? Hardly seems fair."

"I like *him*," she laughed.

"You love *me*."

"True. But you know how it is. This thing between us is new. I don't want to rush it."

"You mean have him find out you're a big geek."

"That too." She sighed. "I really like him, Grey."

"I know you do, honey. And he really likes you. But this isn't the usual start to a relationship, now is it?"

"There is that." They met in July, when she stumbled across a dead body in her neighborhood, and Jonah thought she might have killed the guy. She went from suspect to potential next victim in the blink of an eye, when he turned out to be a wanted criminal from Eastern Europe. Two of his goons tried to kill her, each meeting a sudden and violent end. She still didn't know why.

"How's he feeling, by the way? Is he bored out of his mind yet? Wearing something other than a dark suit?"

"Funny. No suits in physical therapy. He never complains. Pushes himself." Over six weeks ago, her life had turned on its axis again when she witnessed her friend's murder. Jonah had ended up on the wrong side of the bad guy's gun, trying to save her. And Grey.

"Have you had your third date yet?" He didn't even try to hide his laughter. That was Grey code for had they slept together yet.

"The man took a bullet. For me. Some respect wouldn't kill you, you know."

"Exactly my point. He saved your life. The least you could do is give him a little something, something."

"I am not discussing my sex life with you. No matter how much I love you. Talk to you later." She disconnected on his laughter. They hadn't gone there yet, not that he needed to know. Jonah had been shot once, the bullet travelling through his upper arm, wreaking havoc along its path. A nicked artery and fractured humerus had required a trip to the operating room. While she emptied the vending machine and waited.

Two pair of bright eyes appeared at the slider. Followed quickly by yet more nose art, as she like to refer to the smudges the girls left behind. "I'm coming. Hold your fur." She let them in and watched as they ran to their empty dishes. One looked more pathetic than the other. "Who's hungry?" she asked them. As expected, the words set off a hurricane of fur. Both dogs raced around her heels, great herding dogs that they were.

She poured food into each bowl before giving them fresh water. Chuckling as they attacked their food, she left the kitchen to take a shower. She glanced at her phone. Still early at just past eight. Too early to call Jonah. Since being on extended leave, he'd enjoyed sleeping like a 'real person' as he called it. She'd let him rest.

Thirty minutes later, showered, dressed, and itching to get going, Addie let the girls out one more time. As she waited for them to do their business, the opening chords of Thriller, another of Grey's jokes, sounded from her phone. *Jonah!* Sensation zinged through her. She grabbed her phone, sliding a finger across the screen.

"Hey, good morning. You're up early."

"But you sound like you've been up way longer."

His sleep roughened voice sent a frission of sensation down her spine.

"Not way longer. Maybe an hour or so. Just heading out the door in a few." She walked to the glass door and opened it to let the girls back in.

"Let me guess. Off to another estate sale. Nothing else puts that excitement in your voice."

"You do," she replied.

"Good to know. If only I had two good, working arms. I'd show you how I feel about you."

And the zings started in her toes and travelled all throughout her body. "Can I get a raincheck on that?"

"Of course."

The sound of rustling sheets met her ear. She swallowed. Hard. And pictured him lying in bed. And then checked for drool. "Ah, are you still in bed?"

"If I said yes, would you rush over?"

"Would you want me to?" She held her breath, pulse slamming in her throat, waiting for his answer.

"More than you know." He sighed. "How about a proper date? Where we go out to dinner, talk about our days."

"And no discussion of crime or suspects? I'd love that."

"Of course, I can't drive yet. Which means I can't pick you up. So, it won't be a strictly proper date."

"That's the best kind."